Equally proficient in Hindi and English, **Mridula Garg** has written in almost every genre: novels, plays, essays, a memoir, a travel account and ninety short stories. Among other prizes, her novel, *Kathgulab* was awarded the Vyas Samman in 2004 and another, *Miljul Mann*, the Sahitya Akademi Award in 2013. She received the Hellman-Hammet Grant from The Human Rights Watch, New York in 2001. Four of her novels, *Chittacobra, Anitya, Kathgulab* and *Main Aur Main*, have been translated into several Indian and foreign languages. Her essays have been published by leading Indian and foreign journals in Hindi and English. She was the keynote speaker at the UN Colloquium for Women at IOWA and was a Research Associate at UC Berkeley, USA, in 1990.

The
Last Email

~ A Novel ~

Mridula Garg

SPEAKING
TIGER

SPEAKING TIGER PUBLISHING PVT. LTD
4381/4 Ansari Road, Daryaganj,
New Delhi–110002, India

First published by Speaking Tiger 2017

ISBN: 978-93-86338-99-0
eISBN: 978-93-86338-94-5

10 9 8 7 6 5 4 3 2 1

Typeset in Garamond Premier Pro by SÜRYA, New Delhi
Printed at

To the shadow world
Of memories
So agonizingly real

From: anjaliw@womenswriting.com
11 June 2008
Subject: Maya J

Dear Maya,

We received a request for your contact details via our website, www.womenswriting.com from Kevin Wilson. Please see his email below.

Anjali

---------- Forwarded message ----------------

From: K@crossroads.com
Jun 8, 2008
Subject: Maya J
To: womenswriting@gmail.com

I have been reading some of the excellent writings of Maya J. in English translation, and would like to make contact with her again. We were acquainted in India many years ago, but I have lost touch. On your website you offer to pass on any request for contact details. Could you ask her to contact me by email?

With thanks,

Kevin Wilson

M@chaurasta.com to K
14 June 2008

This is unbelievable and a tad frightening. But here's my ID.

`K@crossroads.com to M`
`Jun 14, 2008`

Dear Maya,

We said thirty years—well, it has been forty it seems—but something over the last few weeks has brought you so sharply into my mind and heart, that I had to try to find you, to know you are well and happy. I wrote to the address given on the Jain Samaj website, but heard nothing, then tried other ways!

I have followed your glittering career—you can guess my favourite among your writing, though I regret I can only read in English translation.

If you want to know a bit more of my doings over the long years, try googling me. A few years ago, a grateful (?) government made me a CBE—which anachronistically means 'Commander of the Order of the British Empire'. I am sure you will approve of that!

The years change so many things—but not all.

Kevin

`M@chaurasta.com to K`
`15 June 2008`

Dear K,

We said thirty years—and it is thirty-two since the last time we met, in Delhi in 1976. But of course we first met in 1968, so that way you are right, it's forty years exactly!

I need time to get used to this event...is that the right word?

When did you write? I think Jain Samaj has the correct address. We did shift houses four years ago but are still in Delhi. Can't imagine why your letter did not reach me? Only couriers and special deliveries don't. Bullock-cart mail always does. Maybe your letter came in my absence and was lost or thrown away. I do travel a lot and spent August-September last year in Bangalore as I plan to this year too.

I hate googling, so please tell me what the govt. is grateful to you about? The last thing my govt. is likely to feel for me is gratitude. Well, Commander is not a bad title! So, congrats! Where are you based these days? Not that I am likely to be there.

I passed through London last July on my way to New York for the Vishwa Hindi Sammelan. But except for having a precious book destroyed by security during transit, nothing of note happened. I swore off travelling to the USA—but with an option to change my mind.

This makes no sense. I am babbling. More later; perhaps with more sense in it.

M

K@crossroads.com to M
Jun 15, 2008

Dear Maya,

Are you babbling? I don't think so—but if you are, I love it—and we have a lot of time to make up, so don't stop. It's a pity you're not a googler—it was how I found you again. I wrote about a month ago, to the address on the Jain Samaj website—and I confess I thought maybe you did not want to be in touch again. But I tried again through Anjali W. and here you are!

I know the outline of your brilliant literary history—I would have expected nothing less. But I know nothing of your personal story over the years, and I would like to get to know you again. Your impact on my life was profound and lasting, but I think you know that!

The easiest way of giving you my official history is the
Wikipedia entry about me. That will answer your question
about the stupid CBE. Don't call me Commander—there are
other things I prefer you to call me. The rest of the story can
wait for a while.

M@chaurasta.com to K
16 June, 2008

Dear K,

Ok, I googled, and found you were famous before this mail
arrived. But that does not surprise me. I always thought you
were rather special, in case you have forgotten. Bet you haven't.
Modesty was never your strong point.

'The Reverend Kevin Wilson chaired the executive committee
of the cross-party Constitutional Convention which drew up
the detailed scheme for Scottish Home Rule. It is this scheme
which now forms the basis of the Government's proposals.'

'His dogged persistence in securing consensus through a
series of difficulties drew respect—and occasionally some
irritation—from the participants. He has adhered throughout
to a very Scottish doctrine of popular sovereignty.'

That's great! I particularly enjoyed the idea of your standing
up to Thatcher.

'Thatcherism, according to him, then meant "the end of broad
consensus of British politics."'

'Kevin Wilson said "We have come of age. We are adults not
children. We are citizens not subjects. We are partners not
customers. We are the heirs of a nation that has always prized
freedom above all else. We deserve something better than the
secretive, centralized self-serving super state that the UK has
become."'

'What happens when that other voice we know so well (Thatcher's) says, "We say No and we are the State." Well, "We say Yes and we are the people." That other voice is silent. The State listens.'

I was so impressed by your clarion call 'We say Yes and we are the People.' A simple sentence yet so profound and inspiring! I was reminded of Tilak's saying 'Swaraj is my birthright!'

And of course I totally understand the 'irritation' felt by the other participants along with respect. Makes sense. I believe that respect dawns slowly, only after you have shaken people up by irritating them.

But more importantly, what does retired clergyman mean? That you are no longer a man of God?

My literary career is hardly brilliant. I have deep dark caverns in my life and all my energies go in negotiating them. Writing is one of the weapons and satire the best option. So I have been doing a fortnightly column called Satire in *India Today* Hindi for the last five years.

The strongest emotion I have felt in the past fifteen years—remember we met in 1993 and I lost my son soon afterwards—has been fear. Fear eats into one's soul as nothing else, particularly the fear of happiness.

But before you start feeling tearful, I have survived and will continue to, I guess not because but despite...whatever. Keep sending mail. Goodbye for now. Triviality calls.

Love,

M

`K@crossroads.com to M`
`Jun 16, 2008`

Dearest Maya,

Thanks for your approval and loving comments on my irritating skills at cobbling a compromise! If my head swells a bit more in self praise, you have only yourself to blame!

More importantly, was I special? You certainly were—but the greatest specialness (is there such a word?) was us together. In each other, we became special—and I think, happy, without fear of it.

Anyway, I am in no position to lecture or advise you. I have never known, and can only imagine, the intense pain of losing a child. Your 'dark caverns' trouble me—what does it mean to be afraid of happiness—is happiness not a by-product of relaxing into being ourselves? I wish we could meet face to face—but if there is anything at all you want to share with me, I would be glad to hear and hope to understand.

Was I ever truly a 'man of God'? My faith is unchanged, but I have never adhered to a Christian faith which makes people so heavenly minded that they cease to be earthly. I have never felt or acted very godly—you, of all people, should know that!

As for retired, it just means I have no full-time responsibility any more—but I seem to be doing more than ever, and even a bit of writing—not up to your class, I am sure. But I'm in the process of writing a book called tentatively 'Cosmic Crisis and Creation: The Search for Meaning'.

P.S.: What else of yours can I get in English? I have *Kathgulab (Country of Goodbyes)* and of course *Chittacobra (The Colour of My Being)*. You can imagine my reactions.

K

M@chaurasta.com to K
16 June, 2008

Dear Old Crazy then,

Yes, you were certainly the most un-parson-like parson I had ever met. Not that I had met many. But I remember the other Brit clergyman, Edward I think his name was, in our drama troupe in Durgapur regaling me with a droll account of your un-parson like conduct, including your cutting-edge dancing on board a ship. I can testify to how wonderful and cultivated a dancer you were, while I was lousy. You told me 'just follow me!' That did not work, so you said, 'Ok, do the opposite of what I do.' That worked and we danced. We sure did! When and where: I leave to your memories.

Now, about my books. Do you have *Chittacobra* in English? *The Colour of My Being* was a very bad translation—to the extent that I asked the publisher to remainder it! Which they did, but of course some copies had been sold by then. It was published again in English under the title *Chittacobra*, translated by me this time. I had done the translation earlier and it was put on a floppy by my son. I thought it lost, but eventually found it and the book was published in 2000. But I am mortified if *The Colour of My Being* is the one you read. Do get *Chittacobra*.

Another book you should look out for is *Daffodils on Fire*, a collection of short stories. Anyway, all my books are available to buy online.

My political novel *Anitya* is being translated into English by Oxford University Press. It has been translated a number of times, but never been good enough to be published. Keeping my fingers crossed for this one.

I have just finished the first draft of my new novel in Hindi after a gap of twelve years. And would you believe it, I have written it directly on the computer. I am quite exhausted and am letting it cool before reading it. I am not very computer savvy—only started dabbling in it after 2003, when I was invited to Japan. By the way, Japs are crazy. One example: *Kathgulab* is being translated into Japanese.

You can't even begin to imagine what hearing from you has meant to me. Or maybe you can.

You have still not told me which town you live in. But I don't need to place you at a fixed point. Perhaps it's better to leave it a little nebulous.

About my fear, let it rest for later.

Love,

M

K@crossroads.com to M
Jun 16, 2008

Dear Love,

We danced in Durgapur Club after the play and at the French restaurant at the Taj in Bombay. Those I remember vividly. You were not lousy but certainly a novice—but we soon fixed that, didn't we? I can almost feel you in my arms to the beat of music!

We are in Stratford-upon-Avon now. We shifted here from Scotland in December 1993 to be near our eldest daughter, Liela and her partner. That's what they call them these days. I don't want to be nebulous to you. I want you to feel I am totally real. Does knowing where I live help? I'm so glad you are writing again after twelve years. All power to you!

Love,

K

M@chaurasta.com to K
17 June, 2008

Dearest K,

What made you wait so long to try and find me? And why now? That could be a fair question or maybe it's just a quibble. But it came to mind when I got that impersonal email from Women's World.

Do send me a print of what the museum says about you with photographs if possible! I was in Stratford-upon-Avon for a day in 1988 but despite wanting to, I never made it to Scotland.

It is difficult to exactly say what being in touch with you again has done for me. But, for one thing, my blood pressure has shot up! I feel more alive and more carefree, or careless, or if you please, more selfish. Ah my dear, it is so much easier to talk about books!

I did not say I didn't write for twelve years; I can't survive long without writing. I wrote, but not a novel. *Kathgulab* was published in 1996. I published two collections of short stories and one of travel memoirs between '96 and 2006, but had a block about starting a novel. You know what a writer's block is? It is an excuse for not writing. Or, at best, not hitting upon the right craft, particularly for a novel. At last I chanced upon the right note late one night, two years back, wrote the first twelve chapters in the next sixty-four days—and came to a grinding halt.

By the way, *Chittacobra* was written in twenty-six days and was never revised, but most other novels need to cool. I restarted this one at a snail's pace after a year, and realized last week that it was actually done!

With that kind of a crazy creative process, I try to knock some sense into my days by writing a column and sundry discursive essays. And my travel accounts, though they're not half as exciting as your travels, I'm sure. But, since they include tales about the Maldives, Suriname, Kerala, Nathu La and the crazy Japs, they are not too dull. I can't but recall how envious I used to feel about your roaming round the world.

My new novel is called *Miljul Mann*. I don't know how to translate it in English. Roughly, it will be 'Together in Fantasy'. It is part biography and part fiction, about my elder sister, also a writer, who passed on in 1998. I am told it is quite untranslatable.

Do finish your book. I'd love to read it. Aren't humans always in a state of crisis? It helps to put it in proper perspective. Try me; I won't find it dull. Do you still read Bengali by the way?

And yes, another thing you have done for me is to get me away from the nerve-wracking task of reading my own novel. Ah the joy of playing hooky. Goodbye for now, my love,

Maya

K@crossroads.com to M
Jun 17, 2008

Dear Maya,

Why did I wait so long? It is indeed a fair question, to which I have no convincing answer. All I can say is that something in my heart and mind made me want to reach out to you again. I was determined that we must somehow be together again while we both are still alive and kicking.

You once asked me, after we had made love, to ensure that you would know when I died—and I had asked you for the same promise. Well, I am not ready to wait for that!!

If I might quibble slightly, did you ever try to reach me, apart from 1993? But that indeed hardly matters now.

The important thing is that I hope never to lose touch with you again.

I have found an Indian bookshop in London that seems to have your books—must be a most discriminating bookshop with good taste—and will call in next Tuesday on my way to a conference in Cambridge to collect all I can.

Sorry for misunderstanding about the twelve-year gap—ought to have known that writing is your lifeblood. I am very glad that you have written a novel again, and look forward to reading it one day. Please don't let me be guilty of being a distraction from your tasks as a writer.

More later—I have to dash. My brother Charles is coming shortly from Canada, so I have to do the family thing. As for the museum, I will do my best to send you whatever I can. Will send you a chapter or two of my writing as well—with some trepidation about sending it to a writer as skilled as you.

With my love,

K

M@chaurasta.com to K
18 June 2008

Dear Forgetful One,

Let me remind you, as it is natural that you should forget, since you could not come to meet me. I came to London from Germany and Dubrovnik expressly to try and contact you. That was the year *Chittacobra* had been published in German. As I was invited to Dubrovnik via Frankfurt and my ticket paid for by the ICCR, I managed to get it routed via London. Remember, you were the one who opted out of our relationship. What an ugly word...so American! My letter to you had been returned by the Dead Letter Office.

Anyway, thanks to a persistent if over-zealous telephone operator, who insisted on tracking down your tel. no., though you had shifted from Coventry to Scotland, I found you. I had cold feet by then, but she tracked you down and had us connected. We spoke briefly and you explained that it was impossible for you to come up or down to London. My, were you surprised to hear my voice!

I am not complaining dearest, I fully understand.

It was again on invitation from Germany that I could visit Europe in 1993. I came to London ostensibly to visit my friend L.M. Singhvi, the Indian High Commissioner, but really to try and locate you once, finally.

I did. We met. But...

Why I did not or could not contact you after that is something that opens a wound, I don't know if I can ever talk about it. Some day, perhaps.

Maybe the internet was invented for the express purpose that two crazies like us could communicate and find each other again. Thank God for it!

Bye now. My tea has gone stone-cold.

M

K@crossroads.com to M
Jun 18, 2008

Dear, Dear Maya,

Not only for my forgetfulness, but for any pain I caused you, I am deeply sorry. I never realized that you had come to London expressly to try to contact me, which makes my penitence even worse—I shall have to invest in some sackcloth and ashes. It is even more distressing to hear there were such deep wounds after 1993. I hope you will one day be able to share them with me. Of course, I know of your great loss, but I guess the dark caverns go deeper. Forgive me, and believe that my love for you has never changed.

I was however, always determined that our love should not be allowed to destroy two families. I do remember how your voice sent shivers up and down my spine! The problem with my family remains. I have a wife who is failing and needs me, and three wonderful daughters.

Incidentally, our youngest daughter is doing some work in India for the British Council—she comes out at regular intervals to Delhi and Bombay and is engaged in a project for people in the creative arts, including writing. Do you have any contacts with the British Council? You might ask them about Sheila Wilson—I would love for you to meet her—she knows nothing of us.

More later,

Love,

K

M@chaurasta.com to K
18 June, 2008

Dear K,

I do have some contact with the British Council. In fact, the Women Writer's website was first compiled by them. It has now been taken over by Women's World. I was once invited by them to a conference of South Asian and British writers. I discovered that the Writers' Meet was expressly for promoting and translating fiction written in English to all Indian languages, with hardly any reciprocity. I am not comfortable with that.

I used to be a member of the library during my comfort reading years, in Delhi and in Bangalore. I found that though I could not bear to read works in Hindi, I could in English, which put a greater distance between the protagonists and me. But I am no longer a member...for some years now.

When I joined, they asked me if I had a driver's licence, to check my ID. I said, 'I don't but my driver has; should I call him?' They checked me on the web and I was given the membership but such behaviour does not earn one brownie points.

The point is that I don't have much to do with the Council. Not that they are complaining!

Who knows, someday I might run into Shiela Wilson, the way I did into Gillian W. who, of course, turned out not to be your daughter.

My God I do talk too much! Love

M

K @crossroads.com to M
Jun 18, 2008

Maya,

How can I apologize for us Brits—'perfidious Albion'—but as a Scot, I am sure it was the English in the Council who got it wrong! They always do.

And no, you don't talk too much. I love it, and only wish I could hear and see you as you do!

K

M@chaurasta.com to K
18 June 2008
Subject: Addendum to earlier mail

That conference was when (in 1988) failing to meet you, I took a tour of Stratford-upon-Avon instead. A dead Shakespeare instead of a live Kevin Wilson. Some trade! I also went to Warwickshire Castle and found it so full of things stolen from India that could not help exclaim, 'Castle or robber's den?'— much to the amusement of my fellow travellers, all American of course.

M

K@crossroads.com to M
Jun 18, 2008
Re: Addendum to earlier mail

Dearest,

What a pity you did not find Shakespeare sufficiently stimulating; I wish I had been there to fill the gap! Yes, thank God for the internet. Do you think it was really invented for the likes of us? Certainly the bullock-cart mail, as you so vividly called it, would have made things a lot harder, and probably impossible.

Thanks too, for the news of your new novel, which I may get to read one day. To answer your earlier question, yes, I do still read Bengali, but very poorly I am afraid. I may indeed be forgetful—people often tell me I am—but there are some things I will never forget.

Love, K

P.S. Sorry I made you let the tea go cold

M@chaurasta.com to K
19 June 2008
Subject: Euphoria!

That's the word I was looking for a few days ago. You have brought me to a state of euphoria. M

K@crossroads.com to M
Jun 19, 2008
RE: Euphoria!

Well then—I am thrilled to know how much my contact means to you—you're using words like carefree, and now euphoria. However, my darling Maya, I thought you would have some wonderful totally untranslatable Hindi word to describe your feelings!! Do you? It could be the title of your next novel!

Seriously, I am glad beyond words, and more than a little humbled, by your reaction. I confess I had some fear that you might not want to hear from me again after so long. How can you put up with me again? We ARE crazy.

Tell me more of your feelings, of this 'euphoria' and of what it means to you—I would love to hear it from you, even if I have to imagine your voice saying it, and your wonderful laughter. There is so much I would love to talk to you about—I do hope we can meet again somewhere, sometime—God knows when.

With my love,

Kevin

M@chaurasta.com to K
20 June 2008

Dear K,

Let's say your timing was just right. I had just reached a point in my life when I felt that I needed to live for myself for a while, the littlest while; for one nimish (there's the Hindi word for you). Nimish means a thousandth part of a second, something akin to the atom, but with reference to time. A nimish can last forever in the mind, but for that it has to first happen.

You said writing was my life blood. No, love—it is only a survival kit. Before 1993, I wrote for the ecstasy, because I enjoyed writing; afterwards, I wrote because that was the only way I could survive. My lifeblood was my son whom I lost.

You know, the same event does not mean the same thing to different people. Exile is not equally painful, loss of one's country's independence not equally impossible to live with, loss of a son not equally the end of the world for everyone. It depends on what the axis is, round which one's world moves.

According to the Sufi saints, the real mashooq (beloved) is the son. It was thus for me. A love which is unqualified; never wavers or alters in intensity; includes all other loves; needs no response, yet is fully reciprocated always. Despite the fact that my son had been in love with a girl for eight years, since the age of 18, whom he married in 1992, just nine months before both died together. His love for her included me; mine for him, her. Her love for him included me and all three of us loved each other without qualification, pretence or doubt.

Then it was all over. A meaningless futile death at the hands of a careless, foolish tractor driver on the road and I was not even in Delhi! For the first time in my life I had left home in order to write a novel. I had gone to Varanasi to a friend's house. I completed it, already three-quarters done, at the rate of two lines a day, over the next three years. The 'Vipin' portion in *Kathgulab* was this part, written later.

It was only in 1998 after I lost my writer sister that I could start writing again. She had often said to me, 'What does it matter if you cannot live? Play-act as if you can.' I did. I do. You know how important the family is. I had wanted to preserve it at all cost to my personal happiness—and it was destroyed. My elder son was so traumatized by the accident that he came back with his new wife from USA and was ill for one full year. He recovered, has two children now: a son and a daughter. They say one loves one's grandchildren more than one's children. Sorry, but I don't. My true Mashooqs are still my sons.

Lately, I had started wondering how long I could continue to play-act. And...that was when I heard from you. So...the nimish I needed was there. Now I am going to send this before I change my mind.

M

K@crossroads.com to M
Jun 20, 2008

Dear Maya

You asked why I came to you now. Have you not given me the answer I could not find? I told you, you had come afresh into my mind and heart, and I felt this compulsion to find you. Is it not at least possible that you were somehow calling to me, reaching out to me, over the years and over the miles? Or am I being an incurable romantic? If my rediscovery of you could be the 'nimish' that lasts, I would be happy indeed.

Thanks much more for sharing the depth and intensity of your pain. I want to reach out to you, but there seems so little I can say or do. I want to take you in my arms, feel your tears on my face, and just hold you close—close enough to feel your heart beating. I guess even after all this time, I love you still—and it is a great joy to know that you had not somehow left me behind in your journey through life.

With my love, always

Kevin

M@chaurasta.com to K
21 June 2008

Dear K,

It is fast becoming an obsession. What will we feel if there is no mail for some days, I wonder.

On 27th someone is doing a play based on one part of *Kathgulab,* in Hindi of course. The part he has chosen is 'Aseema', the least complex. But that's how it is, one is best known for the least of one's works. Anyway I am eager to see what he makes of it. I usually do not interfere with the freewheeling interpretation of my stories even when they bug me. I want to allow others the creative freedom I want for myself. But I have the right to feel angry!

Let me explain what 'chittacobra' means. It is not a Hindi word but a coined word made up of the Sanskrit 'chitta' and the English 'cobra'. You must have come across the word chitta in material about Hindu culture. A word common to all the languages of India, including Bengali. It means a little more than the mind or sensibility. So for want of a better English equivalent they used 'being'. Cobra is the snake and is an English word of course. Together they mean a play of colours such as can be found only in the chitta, not in anything of the earth. You can imagine the play of colours in the passage of a cobra through a thick jungle (that of the chitta, but a real one too). As the cobra progresses through thick foliage, its colours are seen in a variegated and unpredictable pattern. Sometimes they are bright, sometimes muted, but always changing and quite indescribable.

Some people mistake it for the Hindi word 'chittcabra' which means dappled. A Bengali is likely to say chittacobra for chittcabra anyway! The German translator called it *Die Gefleckte Kobra*! Not because the translator did not understand the difference, but because he thought the use of the word cobra will make it sell more! The price you pay for being Indian!

I was reading the material on you again. The remark of the Conservative Secretary of State for Scotland that he will jump off the roof if an accord was reached reminded me of the English Viceroy of India who said 'if Tata makes steel, I'll have it for breakfast.' I don't know if Tata ever sent him a piece for breakfast. If the internet was there a century ago, such trivia might have been preserved.

I don't suppose the Secretary for Scotland jumped off the roof either. They never do. That is the difference between the foolhardy Indian Rajputs and other people. I recall my son saying, 'Why do they make such rash promises if they have every intention to keep them!' The story of Indian subjugation.

Anyway I did not quite understand the concept of a devolved English Parliament from the material on you on the web. What would it exactly entail? Do you intend standing for the Scottish Parliament again?

I guess you are doing more important work now, at least by my reckoning. Let me know a little more about yourself. So far it's all been about me.

Love,

M

K@crossroads.com to M
Jun 21, 2008

Dear Maya,

Is it obsession or a kind of intoxication? I too look for your name on my emails and feel a kind of thrill just to see it there.

Thanks for the explanation of 'chittacobra'. Even in the translation you do not like, you can imagine how profoundly moved I was to read it—hope your later translation will affect me even more!

Euphoria, Obsession. Carefree. Lovely words you use. Tell me more of how you feel about me after so long.

And on my part: after the Constitutional Convention (which I chaired) presented its report in 1995, our scheme was for a devolved Parliament for Scotland within the UK. (Incidentally, my book gives a clear account; hope you get to read it soon). In 1997, the Tories were defeated; and the new Labour government called a Referendum to establish a Scottish Parliament. It was held in 1999 and, with a strong vote in favour, it convened in Edinburgh. At its first session, the oldest member said, 'The Scottish Parliament, suspended on the 14th day of March in the year 1707, is hereby reconvened!'

But we are still planning for an Independent Scottish Parliament. Till then, this has ensured that the voice of the people is never ignored again.

What would a devolved English Parliament entail? I suppose it would mean a kind of federal system for the UK, with strong Parliaments in each of the four nations (Scotland, Wales, N. Ireland and England) and a federal parliament for things held in common, such as foreign policy, defence, macro-economic policy, etc. That would mean a radically different kind of Union, based on a written constitution, and much closer to the Scottish tradition of popular sovereignty than to the English concept of the absolute sovereignty of the crown in Parliament. It would mean a genuine and secure sharing of power—at the level of the European Union also.

As for Tata—not only do they make steel, but seem to be gradually eating up some of our industries here for breakfast!

No, I will not stand again for Parliament. I am often called in the media 'the father of the Scottish Parliament'—a title I question because I am on record calling Maggie Thatcher 'the mother of the S.P.' because of her ideological arrogance. I am not too enamoured of the implications!!

On a more serious note, I believe I can negotiate better if I don't belong to a political party. You could say I get a licence to irritate everyone equally by negotiating as an independent irritant.

Sorry the *Kathgulab* play makes you angry. I can't remember you ever being angry when we were together, but that may be just because of the intensity of the other memories I treasure.

Let us not lose touch again

Love,

Kevin

M@chaurasta.com to K
22 June 2008

Dearest Kevin,

Thank you for the explanation. Strangely, the story of the Scottish Parliament makes me feel closer to you, perhaps because it makes you less nebulous. See...politics has its uses, other than that of governing or not letting others govern themselves.

What you said about never seeing me really angry has set me thinking. I have felt for some time that it is a deep-rooted anger in me which is causing me and others much pain.

When did I begin to feel so angry? I always had a quick temper but I was never really angry inside. It was more for the purpose of dealing with the situation at hand.

The play based on *Kathgulab* is a minor issue, if at all. The director is a big shot: Director of the National School of Drama. But this particular bit, being experimental, is not being done by NSD, but by another group. Off Mainstream. The actors are all good. The production likely to be slick and effective. But...I doubt he will maintain my tongue-in-cheek style. He is bound to make it even louder than it is, as the least understated or most overstated (depends on whether the reader likes me as a writer or not) portion of the book. I am merely reserving my right to be angry with his interpretation. But that is an exciting, stimulating, fun type of anger, the earlier kind.

What I feel otherwise is a more serious matter. The first time I felt really angry was in 1984 when the Union Carbide gas leak happened in Bhopal; to the extent that I lost my voice for a while. I had just started writing a column in *Ravivar* (the Hindi edition of *Sunday*) which came out from Calcutta and I used it to give a voice to the activists/protesters. I did not write much fiction between 1984 and 1988. I also joined the Center for Science and Environment which was working for issues connected with ecology. After Anil Aggarwal died, it became like any other affluent NGO. I left its Board in 1995.

I remember asking Anil why he wanted me amidst all the luminaries on the Board. His answer was, 'because you tell the truth'.

The germ of my anger lay in the realization that I could do nothing to help solve the mess, that I was not cut out to be an activist; that I was doomed to tell the truth, with people less and less in a mood to hear it.

It was born, I realize, out of a feeling of helplessness.

It took deep root in 1993. I tried forgiveness to get rid of it. We purchased a small piece of land adjacent to the point on the Delhi-Alwar road—Rewasan was the name of the village—where the accident had happened, with the idea of growing a small forest there. Tapovan or a forest for devotion, we called it. We discovered that the land was not only highly saline but had three other factors needed to make it unfit for cultivation. Still, with the help of a dedicated forest officer and sheer cussedness, we managed to grow some desert trees, which could withstand three months of waterlogging. The extreme salinity of the soil made it impossible for it to soak up the monsoon rain. Our providing drainage did not help, because the entire area for many kilometres around had no drainage and so was waterlogged. The drained water just swirled back. Only the State could help, and it did not...despite the high-flying contacts of CSE.

But we discovered a wild plant called 'dhaincha' which grew in height with the rise in the water level. It was not pretty, but it was green. We built a hut there. The village poor came to rest and fetch potable water, which we bullied the govt. to provide. Most other water there was saline and undrinkable.

All this must be hard for you to imagine. It was for me. With dhaincha and the fire bush and the use of the adage 'don't plan the planting; if a plant sprouts on its own let it be', we saw it turn green enough in five years to attract parrots and Indian nightingales and snakes. Nature provided us with a few wild oleander, shireesh and keekar trees. But my dream of a fruit orchard could never be.

No matter. We opened a small dispensary to give free medicine to TB patients for 6–9 months. TB was rampant there. It was a Muslim village and the people were called Meos. Gandhi lay down on its road after Partition, saying people would leave for Pakistan over his dead body! No one left. Not that they had any intention of doing so. Actually they were converted Rajputs who, though followers of Islam, prided themselves on being the descendants of the warrior king Maharana Pratap. They had readily fought against the Mughal king for him. But we'll let Gandhi take the credit!

But I wanted to talk about forgiveness,

My son had this great quality: he could forgive almost anything. So, to honour him, I tried to forgive. I thought if, one day, the man responsible for his death and for ignoring the cries of his grievously injured wife for help, came to the dispensary for life-saving medicine, my forgiveness will reach fruition. We knew who he was, but there was no point in letting the police proceed against him. He was poor, ignorant and frightened. Also cruel or...just self-preserving. He did come for the medicine, took it and was cured. But...I will be lying if I say I forgave him or the others responsible. Including myself.

When a child dies there is always guilt. Guilt at being alive.

That is when anger took hold of me. I hope my son can forgive me for it. Sometimes I am angry even with him for being on that notoriously accident-prone narrow highway late at night, for letting his novice wife drive, for leaving me behind.

I know anger is counter-productive. That's why I took to writing satire to sublimate it. But I am not rid of it. Far from it.

Why am I telling you all this? I don't know. I haven't shared this burden with anyone. Your saying that you had never seen me angry made me look back and realize...but that's true!

I guess I have to learn to live within my limitations. Recognize I can't change the world. I am not fit to be an activist. All I can do is write a little, not as well as I would like to, but that's alright. One writes what only one can write, not what is good by other people's standards. And I can love. If I can show love and compassion, which is even a hundredth part of the love my son had for all living beings, maybe I can forgive, at least in part and be free of this anger.

Bear the burden of this confession, my love, for love's sake.

Maya

K@crossroads.com to M
Jun 22, 2008

Dearest Maya,

What can I say? I am moved and grateful, for your readiness to share these thoughts, which go so far into the depth of your pain and your struggle. I am frustrated that I can do so little to help you or be with you. As I said before, your openness makes me long to take you in my arms, and somehow share just a little of your sorrow—yes, and of your anger too. Maybe you should be angry with me. Did I not contribute at least a little to messing up your life? There is nothing you cannot share with me—or I with you.

For now, just love,

Kevin

M@chaurasta.com to K
22 June 2008

Dearest,

It's not all sorrow. There has been great happiness too in my life. So many people from all over, not only from India but from France, Italy, Poland, USA, wrote to me, saying my son had touched their lives and that I should be proud to be his mother. As I am. His friends still come to me and, I think, hold me in affection. They often persuade me to join them in their outings when I go to Bangalore, where my elder son has been for the last fifteen years.

I did not mean to make you grieve with me. It is just that you triggered memories and I was faced with the truth about myself. Facing it squarely will perhaps help me deal with my rage. That's good isn't it? I am saved the expense of a shrink!

I don't think you messed up my life. God did it quite by Himself. Anyway that is what life is; always a little messed up but never a total mess. As the Jains say Deh dhare ka dukh hai (the sorrow comes from being born).

Don't worry. Tell me happy things or try perplexities. When feeling real disturbed and depressed, I used to ring up a hardcore Sanskrit scholar and mathematician friend of mine at night and ask him to talk to me. What he said went so much above my head usually that my worries were quite quelled. When I told him I hadn't understood a word he said, he said fine, your job is to write, not indulge in mental gymnastics. So relax. From now on, happy things only.

Love,

Maya

K@crossroads.com to M
Jun 22, 2008

Dearest,

Yes, life is both sorrow and joy, and you certainly seem to have had more than your share of the former, but, I hope, also some of the joy too.

By the way, if our renewed contact helps you enough to save a shrink's expense, maybe I should send you a bill for my usual fee!!

The story of my life... The respectable bits are on the web, and the less so, you know better than anyone else. I remain married, and have three 'dotters' (the way they pronounce it because of my Scottish accent). Leila is Vice Principal of a new Academy in Leicester: Shuba is Principal of the middle school of the international school in Geneva; and Sheila is some kind of high-powered consultant in London, on the creative sector and education—the one doing work for the British Council. They remain close to each other and to us, and your email made me try to imagine what it would have meant if one of them had been taken away.

There is one thing you do not tell me that I long to hear. You were in love with me once. Have I meant anything to you over these years, and what do you honestly feel about me now? I hope I know the answers, but I need you to tell me.

With my love,

Kevin

M@chaurasata.com to K
23 June 2008

Dearest K,

I can only say I must love you still to bare some of my innermost thoughts before you and so soon after we made contact. As if there was no time lag. But there was.

What I have felt over the years is much more complicated. There was the period after 1976, when we met for the last time in Delhi prior to breaking up, in today's parlance. For quite some time I did not believe it to be final. I continued to believe that our love was deeper and more meaningful than the usual affairs and it was equally strong on both sides. Hence, *Chittacobra*! Written in 1979 in just 26 days.

Strange, but in the fitness of things, perhaps, that the first referendum for the Scottish Parliament's devolution should have happened in 1979. Our destinies certainly saw some remarkable coincidences!

Then I began to believe it was indeed over and probably for the best.

After some time, something prompted me to write to you. My letter came back from the Dead letter Office. It left me with an eerie feeling of inconclusiveness and I felt I had to, again in modern parlance, have closure! How easy these glib words make everything sound. But I will not quibble about words, for now.

I tried to contact you in 1988 when I got the opportunity to go to London, primarily to get an answer to the question, you are asking me now; from you and perhaps from myself too. Had your feelings and mine really been as strong and real as I had believed them to be? Or had it been just an affair? No mean thing in itself, but definitely transitory. I had no experience in affairs so could not tell.

After 1988, I think I convinced myself that it had meant much less to you than to me. Also, that it had perhaps meant less to me than I had led myself to believe; fashioning a perfect fantasy out of a reality which was no match for it.

But I suppose, deep inside, I had not given up. So, when a sudden and unexpected invitation found me in Germany with Singhvi's invitation to stay in London, I decided to have one more try at meeting you. The meeting invoked deep feelings, cleared the painful doubt that our love had not meant what we had believed it to mean. The feeling stayed with me when I returned to Delhi but before I could even sift it...everything went blank and remained blank for fifteen years, till your message jolted me out of my imposed memory loss.

So what now?

I think I can safely say that I still love you. That I am content to talk to you through this machine, about my feelings and yours, and feel a thrill I had forgotten.

It is lifegiving to feel body and mind grow into a single entity again.

What I want for now is not to ask questions, not to analyze or sift, but to be. Just be.

So just be.

Is that not enough, my love?

Maya

K@crossroads.com to M
Jun 23, 2008

Yes my love, that is enough—for now. It is both humbling and exciting to know that love can heal, and I cannot but believe I was led back to you at the right time.

Over the long years, you have stayed with me—a kind of permanent presence, sometimes pushed into the background deliberately, but always there. I believe I was determined that I would do nothing more to jeopardize my marriage or family—and somehow believed it would make things worse for both of us if I tried to remain in contact. However, I may be rationalizing to justify myself. Who knows?

What news of your family, after your tragedy. Are you still married—and if so, did that not help you in your journey?

For now, just love,

Kevin

P.S. I will be away on Wednesday and Thursday, back at the old computer on Friday.

`M@chaurasta.com` to `K`
23 June 2008

Yes I am still married. Will write now after 27th.

M

`K@crossroads.com` to `M`
Jun 26, 2008

Maya, Maya, dearest Maya,

Well, here I am, back with my nose to the grindstone! In London, I got your own translation of *Chittacobra* from the Indian bookshop, and have been reading it. The web tells me you were arrested for two pages of the book—which two were they? It all seems so beautiful to me. And what was the outcome of that episode and its effect on you?

I have other questions about the story of Manu and Richard, but they can wait.

The trees are so lovely that the road is no longer barren.

Love,

Kevin

`M@chaurasta.com` to `K`
26 June 2008

I'll write after the preview of the play tomorrow. At the moment I am totally done in. Don't wish me luck, but say break a leg! Love,

M

`K@crossroads.com to M`
`Jun 26, 2008`

OK my love. Break a leg. I'll be thinking of you—let me know how it goes.

Love,

K

`M@chaurasta.com to K`
`28 June 2008`

Dear K,

At last the play is done! It went off well. I love the stage. Wish I was an actor not a writer. They have so much more fun.

Most of the audience wanted me to say that the play did not do justice to my book; that's the 'done' thing you know, which I refused to do. I enjoyed it as a play and was glad to disassociate myself from the novel. I leave it to others to argue about the merit of the production (which was highly experimental), while I enjoy playing blasé.

About the arrest. That is a long sordid story of literary vendetta. The Supreme Court has since quashed the draconian clause of the penal code under which I was charged. I have the dubious honour of being one of the only two writers ever charged under it. There are I believe all kinds of almost never invoked laws in the penal code; clauses they have forgotten to repeal. They are culled sometimes by the enterprising to harass people. Most recently the State of Maharastra charged the *Times of India* with Sedition! They had just remembered the long-forgotten British law!

I had written a light-hearted though true account of it soon after, which was published by the extreme left-wing paper, *Patriot*. I am attaching it. Rather funny isn't it?

The Night I Was Arrested

'There was a knock on my door one Friday evening in 1980, around 9.30. My husband was out of town, servant on leave and two teenaged sons expected back soon from the movies. The knock was followed by an impatient ring. I went to the door, leaving the vegetables simmering on the stove.

Knock at night

Two grown men stood outside. I was about to inform them of my husband's absence, when one of them rasped, "Mridula Garg!"

"Yes."

"You wrote this book?" he asked waving my novel *Chittacobra* at me.

"Why, yes," I exclaimed elated to have my book flashed at me by total strangers. Ah, the ego of a writer!

"Police," said he waving his identity card now. "We are here to arrest you."

"What?"

"Arrest," he repeated, then translated in Hindi for my benefit, "Giraftar."

"I know what arrest means," I said testily, "But what for?"

"The book." He waved it at me again. "Pages 110–112 are obscene."

"They most certainly are not!" I said, so vehemently that he amended his statement to "Legally actionable under The Obscenity Act (U/S 292 IPC)." Obscene? *Chittacobra*!

I recalled the editor of *Saptahik Hindustan* admonishing me for not dwelling more graphically on the sexual act. Also Jainendra, the doyen of Hindi literature, declaring that while reading the novel one ceased to be of the body. I relived the ecstatic state in which I had written the novel. The three "legally actionable" pages dealt with the anguish of a woman who was a mechanical participant in the sexual act with her husband. It was imperative to give a graphic account to emphasize the dichotomy between the mind and the body during intercourse and orgasm. The graphic treatment, in fact, robbed it of erotica, rendering it tedious perhaps, but not titillating.

"What's obscene about them?" I snapped.

"We don't know," moaned the watchdogs of public morality.

"What about scores of other novels dealing with similar subjects?"

"We don't know."

"You don't read books, do you?"

"You don't know how hard it is to arrest a woman when alone"

"I am alone," I said on an impulse.

They blanched and looked at each other. "My God!" I screamed and ran into the kitchen. They followed me, cajoling, "Please, please there is no cause for alarm."

"It's easy for you to say. The vegetables are burnt to cinders and the boys will be home any minute. Guess I'll boil potatoes in the pressure cooker, the quickest thing I can think of." They looked at each other for a long while in silence, then said in unison, quite like Tweedledee and Tweedledum, "Madam, would you kindly get a witness so we can arrest you."

"Just how do you intend to do it?" They went back to looking at each other. "Why don't you go to the living room and work it out while I make tea." By the time I went in with the tea, my boys had returned so we were quite a party.

"Who are they?" asked my sixteen-year-old.

"Policemen. They have come to arrest me."

"Have you killed someone?" asked the fourteen-year-old hopefully.

"No, written a book."

"They can't arrest you for that. What about freedom of expression?" Alas, our schools insist on harping on democracy.

"Apparently they can. They find it obscene."

"Which one?"

"*Chittacobra.*"

At that both of them jumped up. "Are they out of their meagre senses?" They must have looked menacing because the guardians of law cringed as they sang in unison, "Now-now. Please get a witness."

"Here," I pointed to my sons, "are my witnesses."

"They are not adults."

"Nor are those who find literature obscene," said my sons.

"Please," they pleaded, "Get an adult."

"Ok," I said," I'll call my sister."

"No!" they almost shrieked, "Not another woman. Get a man."

"What are you afraid of?"

"Assault and battery. You complaining of them. We mean, women say things and courts believe them. We don't want to arrest you. Our superior officer was after us for a year to get your book but we kept stalling. Finally he got it from the Parliament library and here we are," recited one.

"You are wrong about our not reading books. I have read your stories and don't like the idea of arresting you. But we are helpless," added the other.

"Are you?"

He cleared his throat and mumbled, "Well...actually...we have...er...the discretion to give you bail."

"Here and now?"

"Yes...get an adult male to stand surety and we will bail you. When it goes to court, it's between you, the Delhi Administration and the magistrate."

The aftermath

The adult male was secured, surety signed and I was released on bail. The whole thing had been so farcical that I did not expect it to come up in court. I was wrong. It did and dragged on for two years. Sales of the book were suspended, stocks frozen. That was one of their objectives; the other was to thwart my creative work by causing me mental anguish. Books and writers are persecuted not to stop people from reading but to stop writers from writing freely.

I met the eminent lawyer L.M. Singhvi and asked him two questions: If they considered a part of the book legally actionable, why did they not ban it instead of arresting the author? How was a particular work singled for action when hundreds could fall under the purview of "legally actionable?"

His answers were eye-openers. If a book is banned, he said, the author goes to court and, in case of literary work of unquestioned merit, the ban is usually revoked. An arrest is a greater deterrent as it causes more mental anguish. As for action, it was taken only when a complaint was lodged. The rest was silence, as the administrative officers were not expected to read literature! He also warned me that I was likely to be convicted because I was a woman, perceived as a keeper of public morality.

The Delhi administration confirmed that a complaint had been lodged. The contrite but calm Chief Secretary assured me that the case had been withdrawn, but the police continued to haunt me. I realised that oversight, misplacement, inadvertence were fancy names for inaction. Their eagerness to act and inability to act quickly were so perfectly balanced that the matter remained in perpetual suspension for two years. I must add that before the arrest, a leading Hindi weekly, *Sarika*, had published the three pages, with a letter declaring them obscene and invited "similar" letters. While my male and female colleagues regaled themselves at my expense for a year, as a flurry of scurrilous letters poured in, I was busy writing a historical/political novel, *Anitya*. It was published in 1980. So their second objective that I stop writing was not achieved.

The episode drew to a lingering close in December 1982, the night before it was to come to court, with L.M. Singhvi petitioning the Lt. Governor of Delhi, Jagmohan, to withdraw it, which he did. One may treat the episode as a farce but it raises serious questions, as relevant now as in the 1980s.

Does it befit a democracy to entertain complaints smacking of professional vendetta and act upon them? What kind of law allows unlettered sentinels to witch-hunt authors? Why did most of the literary community remain a silent spectator? Was it because the hunted was a young woman without a male patron?

I firmly believe its silence in 1979 was partly responsible for the latter day witch-hunt of eminent artists, theatre persons and writers. We are quick to blame the right-wing political parties but the rot started much earlier in the bastion of the left.'

M@chaurasta.com to K
28 June 2008

There has been a spate of films recently where two people fall in love via the internet and go on to finally meet etc. etc. We must be the only people in the world who have come to the internet afterwards.

Did you get my book *Daffodils on Fire* also? Two stories in it, 'Daffodils on Fire' and 'A Date With Me' have become more or less synonymous with my name. Read them. You will enjoy them.

I wrote a story called 'Woman of Sixty' when I turned sixty. In it, I referred to the lines in *Chittacobra* that a woman of sixty could do anything she wanted and called the idea utter nonsense. I shall translate it into English and send it to you as a birthday present. I wonder now if a woman of seventy or a man of seventy six is any different... Don't think so.

Lots of people have asked me over the years, particularly young people, for a sequel to *Chittacobra*. I referred them to *Kathgulab*. Poor things! How they'd been had! 'Woman of Sixty' made them feel slightly better.

It's also quite hilarious that no one has ever seen me in the text! Quite surprising considering that women writers are forever lamenting that people read their lives as subtext in their works.

So what about the story of Manu and Richard? You tell me.

Love,

Maya

K@crossroads.com to M
Jun 29, 2008

Dearest Maya,

I am so glad the play went well. If only I was there to see it, and share your reaction, even if I hardly understood a word! Do you remember going to see a play together once in Bombay? I think the same day you gave me your photo 'to the old crazy.' Alas, one I no longer have—but I need no photos to remember you.

Your account of your arrest is a gem. I did not know whether to laugh or cry—so I did a bit of both. Incidentally, it answered my question as to which were the three pages.

The whole of *Chittacobra* moves me beyond words—yes, it is indeed astonishing that nobody ever saw you in it directly.

Really? Nobody? Not even when you wrote about 'the ecstatic state' in which you wrote it in twenty-six days? Maybe the time has come, not thirty but forty years after, to write the sequel, with a new story to tell. Maybe the time has come to reveal the truth about Manu and Richard—it would probably create a minor sensation. Am I serious? I don't know, but part of me would love to live to see it.

If I don't get A 'Woman of Sixty' in English—I will wait impatiently for 'The Woman of Seventy.' Meanwhile I will get *Daffodils on Fire* as soon as I can.

What of Manu and Richard? I am content with Manu's words: 'We merged into one then became two again. But that moment fused into us forever. Ours till death. Till death us do part. We will stay together till death but even if we do not... we...Richard and Manu...that moment of union will remain with us. Till death us do part.'

Love,

Kevin

K@crossroads.com to M
Jun 30, 2008

Maya, Maya,

I still love your name. From the moment we met properly—in a play where I was an old man!!—I knew you were somebody very special! Your lovely accounts, both funny and sad, of your life are fascinating and confirm how special you are. Of course I may be a bit biased, but it seems that, many in the literary world agree. My own life has been dull compared with yours, even if it seemed exciting from the outside. I am keeping your emails in a secret file, so I can read them again. They have come to mean so much to me so quickly.

It is strange that the two pages about Manu and Mahesh caused offence, when those with Richard were so much more intense. I believe—indeed I know—that every man who reads your book would want to be Richard!

Another strange thing. Lodged in the depths of my memory is a remembrance of reading an account seemingly of our last meeting in India, which describes a ferocious, almost violent love-making. Is that memory real? Or is it something I have somehow subconsciously dreamt? I know my memory of the last meeting is real, but did I read about it long ago?

There is so much I long to talk to you about. For now, love,

Kevin

M@chaurasta.com to K
1 July 2008

Dear heart,

Those two pages caused offense not because they were intense or about sex, extra-marital or otherwise, but because every male writer felt offended at Manu turning Mahesh into a body. Had she been thinking of another man during intercourse it would have been acceptable. But she had the temerity to think of abstract things, to indulge in pure thought while engaged in a physical act culminating in orgasm. People are used to men treating women as physical objects but not vice versa. It was unsettling to the male ego.

Much later, when in 1992 the anchor of a program on Doordarshan called *Chittacobra* obscene, I created a major ruckus. My point was: had a participant in the discussion called it that, it would be an individual opinion and could be condoned as freedom of expression. But the spokesperson of the govt. channel had no right to pass judgment on a literary work on behalf of the State. I sent a legal notice which I had drawn up myself to the Director General and threatened to sue Doordarshan, unless an apology was tendered and the producer of the program penalized. This time, the media was with me and I won on both counts without having to sue.

Soon after, I told a gathering of the literati that if the male denizens had problems with my 'description' in *Chittacobra*, all they had to do was to go to their respective wives and ask for an honest take on the matter.

It was not only about *Chittacobra* that no one asked me when and how it was written (except Lothar Lutze!) All my other books were also written in pretty frenzied states, most being done in nine months. Everyone kept out of my way while I was writing. Even *Anitya*, for which I had to hunt and collect banned books, and altogether read about 150 books to get the background of the Independence Movement right, was finished (the first draft at least) in nine months and while the *Chittacobra* case was going on.

I remember when I was writing *Anitya,* my son told me one day, 'Do you know why no one comes to visit us these days? Because you keep talking about 1920, 1930 and 1942 with such intensity that they are scared.'

That's how I wrote.

When the English *Chittacobra* was published in 2000 and I got the Hellman Hammett Grant from the New York Human Rights Watch, *Tehelka* did an interview with me. I don't know whether it's still available on the web. The girl interviewing me, Shoma, did guess the personal angle but agreed not to use it. The young have always been affectionate and protective of me, unlike my contemporaries.

You are right about the account you read. Probably in my story called 'Recantation'. It was written in English and published in *Patriot* first. But I don't see how you could have read it except in the collection *Daffodils on Fire*. But that was first published in 1990. Did you have it at any time?

I really do not understand. But then there is so much I do not understand. As someone said, real love is like a ghost. Everyone talks of it but no one has ever seen it.

Love then,

M

K@crossroads.com to M
Jul 1, 2008

Maya, Maya,

Yes, I can understand the offence to the male ego! I wonder if any of the literati you talked to really took your advice and asked their wives.

I think you were always unsettling to my male ego for different reasons—I prided myself and still do—on always being in control of my emotions! That didn't work, did it?

Your accounts of your experiences are fascinating, and especially your writing and how it was done. I looked up *Tehelka*, and got your article on Delhi—fascinating, especially the bit about *Chittacobra* and Delhi. Was that the interview you meant? And do tell me more about Lothar Lutze.

My memory of how and where I read 'Recantation' is unusually hazy. I only know that I have either read it or been aware of it. Could it be that you somehow shared it with me when we met in 1993? Like you, I do not understand—there is indeed so much I too do not understand, but I know what is real and important. I have treasured surprisingly varied memories of every time we were together. It would be interesting to see if our memories coincide! 'Ah yes, I remember it well'?

You have told me so much, and I seem to have so little to tell of my inner journey. Is there anything you want to ask me? I promise to tell the truth, the whole truth, and nothing but the truth!!

Love,

Kevin

M@chaurasta.com to K

2 July 2008

My love, is there such a thing as the truth, the whole truth and nothing but the truth? I don't think so. Do we ever face the truth without colouring it with a bit of fantasy of our own making? Be that as may (whoever says that!) tell me what you wish to tell me and that will be enough.

One thing though intrigues me. You say you have kept my emails in a secret file. What about my books! Where do you keep them, in a vault?

You know there is no way I would have talked about the account you mention. A couple of my stories were published in USA and were on the net, but not that one. Maybe you had a copy of *Daffodils on Fire* at some time and then...what became of it? I can think of no other way of your seeing it but in the book.

I did not mean the Delhi article. It was a freewheeling interview which went on for the whole day after the Hellman Hammett grant, specifically on the arrest regarding *Chittacobra*. It was on the *Tehelka* website but being news, it must have been taken off after some time. One of the things I said in it was that I write with my womb. That's true. I started writing only after I'd had children, though you had a part to play as well: as catalyst in the whole 'affair'.

Lothar Lutze was the head of the South Asian Studies Institute at Heidelberg University. A Hindi and Sanskrit scholar, he spent many years at the Max Mueller Bhawan in Delhi. He wrote a book called *Postcolonial Literature in India*. The section dealing with Hindi was done around 1980. *Chittacobra* which was published in 1979 had featured in it. He was primarily interested in the creative process, its complexities and technicalities.

Anyway, my life may seem eventful, sad or exciting, whatever, but it was all on a very personal plane. I did not change anything as far as my country or my people were concerned. What does literature do? Exactly nothing! So I definitely feel that it is you, not I, who has achieved something to be proud of; something that can be considered a legacy. A Parliament of your own and your name on the wall of the patriots who made it happen!

By the way, I owe a debt of gratitude to Lynda. She taught music at the Nursery School in Durgapur, attended by my off-beat elder son Ashwin for a year. It was she who told me, 'You have an unusual child. It is up to you to make him abnormal or extraordinary.' Those words stayed with me and helped me deal with a gifted child.

Why she found him unusual makes an interesting story. One day when I went to the Nursery School I found Ashwin sitting all alone in the huge hall which was the Nursery classroom, while all the other children were in the music room singing. I thought he had been punished so I marched up to Lynda and demanded to know why he was not singing.

'Because he doesn't want to,' was her answer.

'Why is he sitting all alone in the classroom,' I demanded.

'Because he wants to,' she replied calmly.

I was furious. 'Are you going to let a three-year-old choose the school curriculum?'

That's when she said her prophetic words.

Interestingly, on D-day Ashwin was in the first row on the stage, singing. Apparently he had learnt the songs while sitting in the other room. Strange but determined!

Later, he decided not to go to school as they kept teaching the same things over and over again and he felt bored. Again the head of the school told me, 'let him not come.' Was I alarmed! I did not want my son to remain illiterate. 'When should I bring him back?' I asked.

'When he wants to come,' I was told.

Great! Let's all be nuts together. I prepared myself to look for another school if I could not persuade him to go to this one, but frankly, I did not want to let it go. It felt special, and secretly, right up my street. I had not attended school myself for three years. Just took the exam and got promoted to the next class. But now I was a mother and supposed to behave responsibly.

Fortunately, after about eight weeks, he suddenly told me one night before going to bed, 'Keep my new suit ready. I am going to school tomorrow.'

So Lynda was proven right and my unusual son went on to get brilliantly educated after all! I wish I could thank her but anyway I have done so, many times during my life. I even told Ashwin and his wife about it. He was too small to remember it happening.

More later. Good night.

M

K@crossroads.com to M
Jul 2, 2008

Dearest Maya,

OK, is there such a thing? 'What is truth, said jesting Pilate, and would not stay for an answer.'

I suppose all our memories are coloured by who and what we are—by our being, maybe. When Jesus said 'I am the truth', he was not speaking of a series of facts, but of something in his person that was love. What we had, Maya—what I hope in some real way we still have—was truth when we looked into each other's eyes and felt somehow completed and at peace. At least, I hope that is how you felt. All I meant was, if you were curious about any part of my life, the outward details, you should ask me.

Your emails are in the file simply because if anything should happen to me, I would not want anybody else to have access to them. Your books are in my study upstairs, in the bookcase. Nobody comes into my study, but if they do, they are welcome to read your wonderful works, which are, after all, in the public domain.

About my book: I wrote it back in 1997—partly the work of the Convention and partly my own story (only the bits that were respectable). Now out of print, but there seem to be some copies on Amazon. I still have one spare copy, and could send it to you if you cannot get it.

Incidentally, I have been racking my feeble brains about 'Recantation'. I think in 1993, after you left, you arranged for me to pick up one your books from the Indian High Commission in London. It must have been *Daffodils on Fire*. Shortly after that, we moved twice, and in one of the moves lost a number of things. That is what I think must be the explanation. I remember nothing more of that book, which I barely had time to read—but that story stayed firmly if rather deeply hidden, in my mind.

Thank you for the appreciation of Lynda. My love for her is real—but somehow so different from ours. I remember

Ashwin...a handsome and distant boy who sometimes looked you straight in the eye. Unnerving!

More later,

Love,

K

M@chaurasta .com to K
3 July 2008

Dearest K,

You know what I really want to do? To have you hold me, lean against you, close my eyes and just be. Beyond play acting, semantics and pretence of being the comforter rather than the one in great need of it. And that is the truth! Touché!

I know it can never be, but mentally perhaps I can conjure it.

So you lost my book in 1993. Never mind. I did more than that. I lost myself.

I am so very tired. I think I will give in to it for tonight.

K@crossroads.com to M
Jul 3, 2008

Yes my love, you can conjure it—and so can I. You are in my arms now, this moment, our bodies pressed together as if holding on to life itself, our faces touching, both wet with tears. Who is comforter and who is comforted?—I don't know. Perhaps we have to be both to be either.

Do we know it will never happen? I prefer to believe that one day, both of us so very different from the lovers we were forty years ago and yet still the same, it might happen.

I hope you are feeling less tired. What can I do, but gently kiss your eyes? Being in touch with you again is bringing back memories that are vivid and full of joy—is it like that for you?

Maya Maya

Kevin

M@chaurasta.com to K
4 July 2008

Yes my love, yes.

And then there were no more words. Only silence. And us. In an all-enveloping serenity. Fatigue melting into untroubled sleep.

M

K@crossroads.com to M
Jul 4, 2008

OK my love—no more words for now—just sharing the silence and us. May you sleep with peace, filled with the memories we share.

Love, K

M@chaurasta.com to K
5 July 2008

Dearest Kevin,

First, here is 'Recantation', which we have talked so much about in our past few mails.

Recantation

'Come to bed with me,' he said bluntly.

She was not shocked. Strange that she was not, considering that it was most unusual. He had never before been insultingly direct like this.

'Take off your clothes,' he said, again in a harsh, almost deliberately hurtful tone. Again, surprisingly, she was not surprised.

She did what he had asked and lay down beside him. He was already on the bed, his eyes fixed above him. He did not turn to look at her even when the mattress sagged and rose to accommodate her. Instantly, he was upon her. There was no tenderness, no foreplay and no urgency. Just a cold possession, a programmed fusion.

Afterwards they lay together, staring at the ceiling. 'I can't meet you anymore,' suddenly he said in a tight harsh voice. Again, she was not surprised. She was expecting this. But she had thought she would be the one to say it. She did not speak, did not ask why. He went on, 'My wife knows about us. She has given me an ultimatum.' She did not need to ask how and what. She too had children and a husband.

She sat up, raised her arms to tie her loose hair in a knot, then lay down again. Now, it was her turn to speak. 'That's alright. In any case, it was becoming increasingly difficult for me to carry on with the affair.' She put an almost imperceptible stress on 'affair'. 'Someday it was bound to come out into the open. It's better to end it now.' Her voice displayed no emotion. Her tone was as harsh as his and her eyes quite vacant.

They lay without more words for a while, then he said, 'What now?'

Suddenly, she laughed, a hard brittle laugh. 'You know what I want?' she asked.

'What?'

'I want you to make love to me.'

He gave a very slight start.

'I know,' she said, 'But I want it the old way, the way you used to. You can be damn good, you know.' Again she laughed.

'So can you,' he countered and gave a laugh to match hers that did not quite match.

'Yes, I always considered myself a good lay,' she said and felt him physically draw back from her. It pleased her. So her crudity has shocked him far more than his abruptness had her.

She did not care to laugh now.

Her hair had come loose again. She drew herself up and raised her arms to gather them back in a knot. She felt his hands on her underarms. Tenderly, they slid to her face and held it cupped like precious porcelain. Yes, that was like old times, gentle, tender and undemanding. She lowered her arms and gave herself up to his soft lover-like caresses with a yielding yearning. They made love as they had hundreds of times before (well, not quite hundreds, around a hundred was more accurate!) She permitted herself a mirthless soundless contortion of laughing lips, but for a fleeting moment only. She let herself go into a kind of trance, in which she could, unquestioningly, believe in the sublimity and depth and undying nature of love.

Time passed.

She started thinking again. It is really quite wonderful that the two of them should still be able to produce and revel in such exquisite sensations. There was a lot to be said for sex after all! She felt she could safely indulge in a bout of satire now that about an hour had passed since the enchantment. She did not mouth it aloud however. Said it to herself with an odd grimace that she was wont to favour when in conversation with herself.

The peace between them was suddenly shattered. He asked in an unneccesarily loud and hard tone, 'So, are you satisfied?'

This time she did cringe under the dull blow but managed to recover quickly and lunge back expertly, 'Oh, quite!' Again she gave a tiny pebble of a laugh. Really she is much better at laughing than he is!

'I'm glad,' he said, 'my reputation was at stake.'

'Do you want me to give you a job satisfaction certificate or go and have a chow with your next conquest?'

'No,' he laughed, but again, it was not quite as well done as hers. 'I don't propose to keep you informed.' She got out of bed and started putting on her clothes. 'You must not worry. Having short affairs is quite safe,' she threw over her shoulder, 'No one is likely to find out. It's only when they drag on that a scandal becomes more or less inevitable.'

'So, keep them short,' he said flatly.

'Exactly!' She gave a pause, then said in a more challenging tone that she had hitherto employed, 'You don't care to risk the scandal with subsequent high jinks of broken homes and all that, do you?'

'No,' he said.

'Nor do I,' she countered, and this time decided against a laugh.

A little more time passed.

She was fully dressed and made-up now. A trifle too made up, he thought fleetingly as he looked at her in the dim light of the curtained room. He could not see her clearly for long. His vision was strangely blurred.

'How about a last drink together?' she drawled. 'Don't bother to get up. You look quite beautiful from up here.' She bent down, kissed him lightly on the cheek, discounted the tang of salt on her lips and walked to the sideboard with steady steps. She prepared the drinks carefully and brought them to the bed.

'To us, the eternal lovers,' she said with a hard laugh and clinked glasses with him.

He did not say anything but downed the drink in a sort of a defiant gulp. She finished her drink with slow deliberation and walked out, erect, head held high, cool and composed.

She glided down to the lift and got in. It went down. She did not get out in the lobby. The lift emptied and then filled again. This time it slid up. She rode it to the fourteenth floor rooftop and got out, very erect, looking straight ahead. Without a care she walked to the edge of the terrace and very deliberately threw herself down.

There was a lot of commotion. Doors banged. Women screamed. People ran here and there shouting bloody murder. But he remained undisturbed. Totally unaware in fact.

He did not leave the bed after she walked out. He lay on his back staring at the blur of a ceiling. He had a confused dream in which he made love to her in absolute soundlessness, then drifted into a very sound sleep indeed.

K@crossroads.com to M
Jul 5, 2008

Your story has left me gasping. Yes, this is the one. Though I didn't remember the ferocious details, I had a fairly strong recollection of the incandescent feelings expressed in it. But I wasn't prepared for the full burst of passion shown by the lovers, and the fitting, though brutal, end. I feel both humbled and blessed to be reminded of this raw passion. When did you write it? No, don't tell me. I know you wrote it soon after I left India. But let me assure you, dearest Maya, that the passion still abides with me...or shall I say, with us...

M@chaurasta.com to K
6 July 2008

You are right. I wrote it soon after you first broke up with
me. 'Breaking up' sounds so American. But never mind. I
was as distraught as I was angry at that time and the end
was fashioned out of that. When I read it again, now, while
sending it to you, the violence of the passion made me feel a
bit foolish and I almost didn't send it. But deep down, I too
felt both humbled and exalted to have known such passion.

And now, dear love, let me make you feel a little less breathless
(me too). So, to catching our breaths back and being done
with recantations of various kinds. I want to recall some of
the fun things we did together and put the burden of this
violence behind us—but not the passion. As you say, it still
abides with us.

I remember well the play we saw together in Bombay where
we were the only two people in the hall! Strangely enough,
last night the name suddenly flashed through my brain. *The
Professor Has His War Cry*. You will be amused to know that
the chap responsible for the entire play, writer-director-actor-
dancer, one Pratap Sharma, later did a few good things on the
stage and screen.

In fact, I ran into him when he was acting in a film based on
Jainendra's *Tyagpatra*. Jainendra was the doyen and iconoclast
of Hindi literature and also the only one who had stood up
for *Chittacobra*. I happened to be there during his meeting
with this young man, in the late seventies. I burst out laughing
when he was introduced to me. I felt sorry and in mitigation
explained that I had, along with a friend, been his only
audience at his play in a college hall. Sophia's! It has just come
to me. It only made matters worse but he was a feisty young
man. He laughed and looked rather quizzically at me. I also

remember now that we had some bad tea during the interval but I did not tell him that.

The film unfortunately flopped, as did the one they made on a story of mine. But naturally! Art films! Who sees them! In fact, I hated the one they made on mine, though Jainendra said it was good. I returned the compliment, but we both knew the box office was jolly well going to reject them. Nothing more was heard of Pratap Sharma—unless he is famous under some other name.

I don't remember giving you a photo of mine that day, though I do remember you taking one of mine which must still be there, somewhere. I also remember visiting Land's End in Bombay with you. I did not know its name then. It was told to me later by a Mumbaikar when I described the place to him.

There must be so many memories we both remember. Though there are some I had blanked out, like leaving my book with the High Commission. I am cursed with a good memory. It can be really painful at times, but a blessing at others. So a toast to shared memories!

Remind me of other memories you have. Let me see what I can add to them. Love and love again and evermore, God I sound like a B-grade movie but I'll let it go.

Maya

K@crossroads.com to M
Jul 5, 2008

Maya Maya,

Memories—yes.

Of the play in Bombay I remember little, except the joy and fun of being there with you, and the fact that we were the only audience. Loved your story of meeting the author long after!

Land's End in Bombay? That is one I do not remember. What was it and what did we do there? I remember you taking me to a hotel outside the city for a night—when I was still at the frustrating stage of longing to be with you, but at the same time hesitant, and maybe afraid to take the final act of total commitment.

Anyway, that leads me to one of my most intense memories— the first time we fully consummated our love. I can remember where we were and how it happened, and the glorious feeling of being with you. Perhaps you remember it too. If you want, I could remind you! Maybe one unforgettable memory is enough at a time? But there are many more!

Never mind the B-grade movie. I love it. I love you.

K

M@chaurasta.com to K
5 July 2008

The hotel was Sun and Sand at Juhu Beach. Just before we went to see the play I got my short hair done in a bun by the hair stylist there, because you wanted to see how I had looked before you met me. No wonder I inscribed the photo I gave you, 'To the old crazy.'

You took a photo of mine standing next to a lamp post in that bun—French roll she had called it, ugh! It was not very good technically but the silhouette was rather fetching. At least that's what my sister said, when she chanced upon it in my album.

Now when did we go to the Land's End? It is a point somewhere near Juhu, so I guess we must have wandered there on our way to Sophia to see the play. I haven't been to Bombay for so long, the landscape has changed beyond recognition. But I do remember asking my friend, in 1990, about this point in Bombay, where suddenly the city seemed to disappear and there was nothing beyond. I wasn't sure whether it was real or I had dreamt it. But when he immediately said Land's End, I felt vindicated. The context is very hazy but the view is quite vivid in my memory.

I need no reminder of the memory you are talking about.

I discovered very early that the best way to keep things hidden was to put them right out in the open. No one then bothered to look beyond their noses. That was why no one saw me in *Chittacobra*. Even when out of contrariness, I sometimes told people that I did not need to write an autobiography because my book was largely autobiographical, they just laughed as if I had made a huge joke.

Looking back, I feel I was very naive. I had no experience in conducting an extra-marital affair. I was wary of commitment and its consequences. Had I been sixty then I would have been much more forthcoming! But had I been sixty then, nothing at all might have happened. Ah choices! Choices!

Goodnight for now, its 10.30.

Love

M

K@crossroads.com to M
Jul 6, 2008

Dearest

Had you no experience in an extra-marital affair? I, of course, had had 51 before!!

In what way do you reckon you were naive—or more so than me?

I can look back over the years, and say with complete assurance that there is nothing in our times together that I would change for anything in the world. My only regret is that, given the commitment we both had, it had to end.

'Non, je ne regrette rien'

I only vaguely remember the Land's End—I think at that stage I was so intoxicated with you, I may not have taken everything in. I do remember the bun! Do you still have that photo in your album, my love? I am sure the silhouette must have been fetching indeed!

Do you remember the exact moment when we first met? I cannot be sure, but most clearly remember the play in Durgapur in which you were asked where you had kissed someone, and answered, 'On the lips.' I remember thinking you breathtakingly beautiful and hoping against hope we could at least be friends. Who was I kidding? Somewhere I still have a recording on an old tape of you saying those three words, which I must have recorded at a rehearsal. Choices indeed!

Love,

Kevin

M@chaurasta.com to K
7 July 2008

Dear Heart,

No, I don't remember that line though I remember the play in general as a place where we met. But no, I can't pinpoint the exact first moment. I remember something rather droll—I kept calling you Kemin instead of Kevin and you never corrected me.

I particularly remember a car ride to some place close to Durgapur, where we had gone to do the play. A second performance or a rehearsal. The two of us had sped off in a car leaving the others behind. Later the other Brit, Edward, gave me some solemn advice to keep away from you.

I also recall strolling with another woman (don't remember who) in front of you during a rehearsal (quite like *Pride and Prejudice*) to attract your attention. Which, of course we did, soon enough.

And I remember you giving me a foot massage. I am talking of very early days of our meeting. I loved it. My feet have always been rather demanding of attention. Even now. That's a memory that has come to me unbidden so many times during the last years.

I am leaving for Bangalore on 3rd August and will be there for a month or so. I have access to my email there. Maybe I'll translate 'Woman of Sixty' and send it to you.

If you don't know in what way I was naive, then you are being naive now. Anyway here is a poem I wrote a long time ago. Naïve, maybe but expressive.

No More

I loved a man once
Even as I lay in his arms
I remember I wept for today
Ecstasy stilled
Ache assuaged
Gap filled
With a thousand trivial cares

False love?
Yet in the lengthening shadows
Of the night
Another shadow takes shape
The shadow of a memory
The memory of a memory
Of a point of light
That pierced my being
I open my arms
Renew the ache
Dismiss the commonplace
Ecstasy stirs like a new born
It goes the way of all shadows
Lengthening out of my arms
Faint blurred no more

Did I show it to you earlier? Maybe I did. I don't even remember when I wrote it. Found it in a lot of old newspaper cuttings and things.

Goodnight now, my 52nd affair.

Maya

K@crossroads.com to M
Jul 7, 2008

Dearest Maya,

Your poem is beautiful and, for me, deeply moving. If I had ever seen it before, I am sure I would have remembered... When did you write it? Any more where this came from—your heart?

Did you call me Kemin? That I had forgotten. When did I eventually put you right? (I mean about the name—not in general!) You, my love, can call me anything that takes your fancy. Certainly by the time you said my name in the way and at the time I loved best, you had it right!

Of the play I remember nothing, except you—and I can hear your voice now. The incident in the car I do remember—also what we did in the back seat. I remember massaging your feet—they were lovely—just like the rest of you. Life might have been simpler if you had heeded Edward's warning—or if you had not walked in front of me to attract my attention. Boy, did you succeed!

I would love to get 'Woman of Sixty', especially since I did not keep what I think was my promise to contact you then. Why did I have to wait ten more years?

I look impatiently for your name on my list of new emails.

Love,

Kevin

By the way, the other 51 must have been totally useless. I can remember nothing of them!

M@chaurasta.com to K
8 July 2008

My love,

I go to Bangalore because my elder son Ashwin and his family are there. This is my only family. Also I have to be in Trivandrum on 14th Sept. for the release of the Malyalam translation of *Kathgulab*.

I desperately need this time off from the household to recharge my batteries. The moment I reach Bangalore, I begin to sleep well and late into the morning. Since I am in granny mode, I go back to cooking goodies and being a confidante of my granddaughter, who is a fine actor and a budding writer, though only ten.

Apart from this yearly sojourn, every other place I go is for work. Not bad. I get to see places and feed my ego, but it remains stressful. This is pure pleasure. I go at a time when Delhi is muggy and hot, while Bangalore is lovely, weather wise and otherwise. Summer vacation is over, so everyone is out during the day at work or school. I am alone to read, sleep, cook and write. Evenings are family time, as are weekends. An ideal situation.

I don't remember exactly when I wrote that poem. I haven't written any since 1980 so it must have been before that. There should be a few more. I'll send them if and when I can lay hands on them.

Love,

M

K@crossroads.com to M
Jul 8, 2008

Maya, Maya,

Your description of your family time in Bangalore made me understand how it is a time of real rest and renewal. Interesting too that *Kathgulab* is in Malayalam—I always thought while listening to Malayalam that it was like a rushing river in full spate!

On Thursday (10th) I am off to Edinburgh for the launch of the new unit at the National Museum of Scotland. It is called 'Scotland, A Changing Nation', and the section on political change features yours truly. It will be opened by Scotland's First Minister Alex Salmond. So, I will be away from my computer for a few days over the weekend. If you have never been in Scotland, maybe it is time you were! After all, you carry a little bit of Scotland in you—forever. If you ever do come, I will be there.

If you find any more poems, please do send them.

Love,

K

`M@chaurasta.com to K`
`8 July 2008`

Is there a wax sculpture of you?

`K@crossroads.com to M`
`Jul 9, 2008`

Dear one,

Why do you want a wax sculpture—to stick pins in it?

Sheila, the daughter I am closest to, is coming with me up to Edinburgh tomorrow—she was in Bombay, (Mumbai is more PC) and Delhi on British Council work. I am resisting the temptation to give her *Chittacobra* and ask what she thinks of it. Don't worry, I won't— but I would dearly love to. Something in me wants to say that I am unashamed, indeed proud, of what are some of the most precious memories of my life.

I do have a little gripe about this name changing—Kolkata and Chennai and Mumbai and all the rest. My middle daughter lives in a city we call Geneva—its citizens call it either Geneve or Genf, depending on whether they are French or German speaking. The same is true of Cologne (Koln in German) or Basle (Basel) or a host of other cities. I feel no compulsion to change the English versions of these names to bring them in line with their home names. So, by this logic, why should I not call them Bombay or Calcutta, while happily accepting that in their own languages their name is somewhat different?

That is what I do all the time with other places. When I read the flight board for the plane I am about to board in London, I expect to see 'Cologne'—but when I land, the airport sign informs me I am in 'Koln'.

I was unsure about letting loose this diatribe on you. But I would like your opinion. Oh, and one other question: I have not yet understood how Madras became Chennai?

There is a line at the end of one of your stories that troubles me a lot. More than 'Recantation' does. Come to think of it, 'Recantation' did not trouble me after the initial jolt—it moved me intensely. But this line, when you say 'after all, there is no point in anything anyway' troubles me.

My love, my dear love, that does not sound like the Maya I know and love so dearly.

Your life has had much more sorrow than mine, but I am very deeply saddened by that one throwaway line. Of course there is a point, even if we do not fully see it at the time. Certainly I feel that our contact again after all these long years has a point.

If you answer this, I will get it only on Saturday afternoon when I get back—I decided not to spend the whole weekend away.

Did I tell you that when I was trying to track you down through the internet, I came across another Maya J, who seems to some kind of high-powered mathematician? I almost tried her in case you had changed professions!! Who knows, she might have been the 53rd!

I remember your laughter—do tell me you have not forgotten how to laugh.

With my love,

K

K@crossroads.com to M
Jul 9, 2008

P.S. After I wrote I realized that I will be leaving home at 9.30 tomorrow morning—which will be something like early afternoon for you—so if you get a chance to reply, I could get it before I go—would send me off with the warm glow I always get from your emails.

Love again.

M@chaurasta.com to K
9 July 2008

Dearest,

There is a point to life, oh yes, definitely, and then there is not. I veer from one state of mind to another. Somewhat like Madras and Chennai. Is it the one or the other—and does it matter? Sorry for the pop philosophy. But this I will grant you: our contact again after all these long years has a point.

If only to allow me to enlighten you about the conundrum of Madras and Chennai.

The question to ask is not how Madras became Chennai but how Chennai became Madras. I was always intrigued by the total dissimilarity till the matter was clarified by my Tamil friend. He is an arrogant intellectual snob as only a South Indian Brahmin can be, but quite Westernized in his intellectual beliefs. Anti-Hindi (chauvinist, he calls it) despite being proficient in Hindi, perhaps more than I. This preamble is to indicate that the story he told me was not because of, but despite, his bias.

It seems there was a barber called Madaraasan who became a special pet of the Viceroy while in Chennai. So it was decided to rename Chennai, Madras after the 'noble' barber, something like a knighthood I guess.

For myself, I don't mind the names being changed back to the original meaningful and musical ones. I quite like it. The new names are so much more aesthetic.

I have Amitav Ghosh on my side. We don't mind people who cannot pronounce the new words calling the cities by the British names; only it is so very dull. Delhi has absolutely no resonance for me whereas Dilli is like a strain of lilting music. It reminds me of what an American once said to me: could he call me Muriel? Certainly not! Better call me Madam! Or Sir?

Wax sculpture? Oh, I meant you might be in Madame Tussaud's Museum.

Bye now,

M

K@crossroads.com to M
Jul 9, 2008

Dearest Muriel,

That was just to annoy you! As you no doubt remember, I have never had any difficulty saying your name—but if I did I would just call you Manu. Somehow, *Chittacobra* would not have worked so well with Muriel and Kemin!

Fascinating about Chennai. I suppose we should be grateful the barber was not called Shivaramakrishnan like my South Indian friend in Durgapur. I take your point about the poetry and lilt in the names—so I shall call them whatever you do!

Sleep well my love,

Kevin

K@crossroads.com to M
Jul 12, 2008

Dearest Maya,

Back home—all went well. I did not make a speech—pity they were deprived of my wit and wisdom—and the First Minister was represented, as politicians tend to be, by the Minister for Culture who made a good speech. You showed me Delhi—with new eyes—maybe one day I can show you Scotland.

Keep your faith in love and your hope for the future.

Love,

K

M@chaurasta.com to K
12 July 2008

Dearest,

Read about you on the web in a piece on the opening of the National History of Scotland section of the Scottish Museum. I am thrilled. But tell me more and do send me the book.

M

K@crossroads.com to M
Jul 12, 2008

Dear one,

Glad you approve. After all, if India can throw off the English yoke, why not Scotland—though I have to admit Scots were in the forefront of empire, but that was only because we are so much more capable!! We still have to finish the job, but I have made my small contribution. Did you read the article in today's *Scotsman* newspaper, which gives the exhibition's text for ten people, including me? If not, google in *The Scotsman* and my name and see if you can get it.

It is not (I hope) immodest to say that both of us have made an impact in our different ways on the human story—not to mention our impact on each other!

You say 'tell me more.' What would you like to know? I am halfway through writing a book on the current human crisis, and the Christian understanding of it based on relationships, called provisionally 'Healing the Nations; Healing the Earth.'

With my love,

K

M@chaurasta.com to K
13 July 2008

I'll google and see if I get you.

Meanwhile I am having some problem with my stone-age computer, so if suddenly you don't hear from me for some time keep faith. My instinctive reaction to a computer failure is to pray. As I did just now and it did start.

Funnily enough, when I had my first interface with computers, which was in US—my son was there in Silicon Valley and I had been invited by the South Asian Studies Department of UC Berkeley—wherever I went, whether my son's house, another friend's house or Berkeley, there was a system failure! My son blamed it on my lack of faith in the computer and called it, its intelligent revenge. I was quite mortified as he is the ultimate computer wizard.

The S.A. chief, a Sanskrit scholar, told me I better chant mantras to take away my negative influence on the machine for after all, mantras were the original software. The Brahamastra in the Mahabharata (reckoned to be a guided missile) was the hardware and the mantra, the software meant to make it work. Because Karna forgot the mantra at the crucial moment, he could not operate the weapon. There is more to it. Arjun refrained from using it fearing the holocaust it would cause, while Ashvathama used it, causing wholesale carnage and was then condemned to immortality.

Anyway the point is that since I consider my son guru material, I tried to do away with my negative vibes re: any machine particularly a computer and here I am. For me to be able to operate a computer, even to the extent of using it as a word processor, is a major victory of mind over matter, or rather, mind over mind. Not bad then, is it, that I have managed to write an entire novel straight away on the computer without first doing it by hand, as I had my earlier books.

But like Nietzsche (he said it about the typewriter) I feel it changes the way one thinks and the only reason I could do this new novel on it was because it had a craft which suited the word processor or vice versa.

But even now, faced with a blink all I do is chant mantras!

Meanwhile here's another poem, in case my prayers are not answered by whichever god looks after computers.

Love and all that goes with it,

Maya

`K@crossroads.com to M`
`Jul 13, 2008`

Thanks my love, for another beautiful poem—was that also from long ago, or are you still writing like this?

Your computer skills, or lack of them, reflect mine—I can just about use word processing and emails, but most of the rest is a mystery I do not expect ever to probe. On the other hand, I do not seem actually to affect them adversely just by being around. You must have a very special kind of electricity—but then I always knew that!

The *Scotsman* article describes ten people who are featured in the new gallery. Apart from any interest you might have in No 8, I thought all ten might interest you as giving something of a glimpse of Scotland—so I hope I can send it as an attachment to this email.

Must rush—so just love for now,

K

`M@chaurasta.com to K`
`14 July 2008`

Thanks dear for the attachment. Unfortunately, an error occurs while opening the Google document. So my dear love, you too seem to have an adverse effect on the internet. Bad company, I guess! Please send me the book. Amazon does not seem to like me! And the computer has fresh torments for me.

Suddenly, the date on my computer jumped to 2090 when I typed Kevin Wilson on the google and everything went haywire. The internet won't open, saying security had been breached! I rang up Ashwin, which I always do and got the stock answer, 'Computers are designed for the IQ of an idiot. Keep reading what it has to say and you will get it.' He is ever so inspiring!

I was fuming and bent upon proving I was no idiot. And sure enough, the computer told me to set the time and date on the control panel. Never dreaming it was not the date that had changed but the year itself, it took me hours of sheer pig headed fiddling to decipher it. Finally I got it! Was I happy!

But when I tried to get you out of the attachment you sent me, it kept saying Error. So my love, the computer obviously has reservations about you and me.

M@chaurasta.com to K
14 July 2008

Ah, finally the Computer God answered and I could open the attachment and read about all you luminaries. But I must confess, I was self-obsessed enough to concentrate on you, and give the others a cursory glance. That does not mean that I do not endorse fully an Independent Scotland and sovereignty of the people. I would have anyway, but not as passionately as now—because you fought for it.

What you say is so right. Here it is with my comments!

"'LIFE must be lived forward, but understood backward," said philosopher Kierkegaard.'

You are fond of that quotation aren't you? I remember hearing it before.

'As I look back on a long and exciting life, I can see a clear pattern and purpose that were not evident at the time. Each stage was important in itself, but each was also a preparation for what was to come. My years in India taught me that poverty is neither accidental nor deserved, but the direct result of our economic and political systems.'

How absolutely right! Unfortunately the rich and powerful have the myopic vision to think that it is in their interest to keep people in poverty. So...it goes on getting worse.

'*As director of Coventry Cathedral's Centre for International Reconciliation I learned about the patient, painstaking work of bringing people together across divisions, to "heal the wounds of history". These were, I believe, the gifts of experience that I brought to the Constitutional Convention, to steer through stormy waters and a series of minor miracles, to succeed where so many had failed before. We have a Scottish Parliament at long last.*'

Not that your negotiating skills were ever in question. After all, you negotiated my secret desire for passionate love without a demur and lot of passion. Not that I made it hard to negotiate...I am mighty glad that you also have a Scottish Parliament at long last and not just me!

Take your time to reply to this. No rush. I know I shot off a number of mails yesterday in the process of trying to prove my son wrong, or right, whichever. He always has this effect on me. Unlike my other son, who filled me with serenity. But I love them both equally. Two faces of love. One prickly, disturbing and challenging; the other, tender, forgiving, serene.

The poem I sent you is from before 1980. I have never published my poems, except two in the beginning. Recently, some research students persuaded me to trace the forgotten pieces and that's how they are on my computer. Anyway... you know the kind of thing I write these days... Country of Goodbyes!

Love,

Maya

K@crossroads.com to M
Jul 14, 2008

Dear M,

You should write up your account of your struggles with the recalcitrant computer and publish it. Maybe the internet has decided our emails are too interesting and is trying to get in on the act. Maybe we should make them even more interesting by including a few of our more intimate memories of each other?

Glad you got the *Scotsman* article. Now all you have to do is get to Edinburgh to see the exhibition.

So for now, I just say your name—Maya, Maya,

K

M@chaurasta.com to K
15 July 2008

Dearest,

I might have told you I write a piece of satire every fortnight for *India Today* (Hindi). So I use all such material for my obligatory humour column. In fact, that is my bread and butter, since writing fiction in India hardly earns anything. Writers traditionally are supposed to live on tea and love. Of course, I write in Hindi and the pieces are never translated into English. So I have only you to practice my English transgressions! Might help me improve my command over the language. Something I'm never quite sure of.

Ah, you want to leave an interesting legacy to people. The best way to do it is to leave your secret file to a dear friend, the dearer the better, and ask him to promise solemnly to destroy it after your death. That is sure to make him want to go public with it. You can rest easy that all shall be known to all. That is what Kafka's friend did with his literary pieces and Felice did with his letters to her. She was a smart cookie, so she did it in her lifetime and made a sizeable amount of money. Nothing makes people want to disclose things more than being told expressly not to.

The rain has stopped for a while. I think I'll go for a walk. Good night,

Maya

K@crossroads.com to M
Jul 15, 2008

Dearest M,

Hope you had a good walk. It is hot and sticky here today, reminds me of Calcutta (sorry, Kolkata), so I will go for a walk later. As my daughters say, TMI (Too Much Information!)

I can imagine your satirical writings, and just wish they were in English so I could read them. Of course, it would be a great honour to be the one on whom you practice your English, though I strongly suspect that your English is better than mine! Anyway, I cannot promise you any fee— though I can supply the tea, and certainly the love.

Why don't you write the next part in the story of Manu and Richard, possibly in the form of correspondence, with enough clues to let the perceptive reader guess what is happening— and send it me, making me promise to destroy it!! On second thoughts, that might be too tempting.

Glad your computer is behaving, for I love receiving your emails.

Love,

Kevin

M@chaurasta.com to K
16 July 2008

What's wrong with TMI? It's good to know the small details.

Do you remember the day we spent together in Calcutta way back when we were both in Durgapur? I even got my hair cut there—why, I can't imagine, except that Durgapur did not offer the facility.

I was in Kolkata (I call it one or the other as the mood takes me) last year in October and I passed a place called 16 Sudder Street. Wasn't that address associated with you in some way? I was staying at the Ramakrishna Mission Guest House and went out for some shopping and coffee and don't know how and where I passed that address. I was on foot. It rang a bell but it was only last night after you mentioned Calcutta that the day spent with you there suddenly came to mind, full blown. See the power of TMI.

Love,

M

K@crossroads.com to M
Jul 16, 2008

Yes I remember the day in Calcutta—I think I remember every day we spent together—but I can only remember one night in Bombay. Am I right? Tell me what else you remember about the day in Calcutta, please.

Yes, you should remember 16 Sudder Street. It is where I lived briefly before coming back to Durgapur. More important, it is the address where Richard picked up his mail!! So it should indeed ring a few bells!

This contact is awakening a flood of intense memories—never forgotten, but maybe quietly sleeping in the background. Is it for you?

Love,

K

M@chaurasta.com to K
16 July 2008

Park Hotel in Calcutta! Was it the newly built Park Hotel on Park Street we went to? Yes! I think it was.

When I got my hair cut rather short you said, 'what a pity all that lovely hair has to go. But I'm glad because I can see your earlobes now.' Silly thing to say or was it?

Yes there was just that one night in Bombay.

We always met in cities swarming with my family. And the children were small. I needed to keep in touch to find out whether the kids were fine. So getting out at night was not possible. By the time I had started travelling and could meet you anywhere in the world, we had broken up, parted, could not meet...what would be the correct term, I don't know.

So guess we were star-crossed lovers. Well, that's what lovers are supposed to be, my love.

K@crossroads.com to M
Jul 16, 2008

Yes, yes, it was the Park Hotel in Park Street—and I do remember your hair. Your ears were lovely and I wanted to kiss them. I hope I did! I remember much more than your ears—but something in both of us prevented us from completing our love then, and for some time after. But I do remember the first time we did—the Taj in Bombay. Am I right my love?

Are we star-crossed lovers? I suppose we are. I have a firm conviction that our love would have lasted as long as we allowed it to. Indeed, the way I feel now, it has not gone away.

Love,

K

M@chaurasta.com to K
17 July 2008

My darling,

Bombay and Taj evoke memories of the most intense moments of our being together. But memories are tricky things. One can't be selective about them when they come rushing back, as one can in a novel.

If you mean what you say that our love would have lasted as long as we allowed it to, then I have to ask what exactly happened to make you disallow it so completely when you did.

But above all, tell me, when did you actually read *Chittacobra*? Did it have something to do with your deciding to contact me after so long? I need to know this.

More later,

M

K@crossroads.com to M
Jul 17, 2008

Dearest Maya,

Memories are indeed selective—but my memories of being with you are fresh again and detailed, as I think they are for you, from your reference to the intense moments. I think I could describe to you all these moments, from stolen kisses in the jungles of Durgapur to the glory of Bombay and Delhi.

Why did I think, with deep sorrow, it had to end? I suppose I had come to the feeling that we could not go on with occasional meetings God knows where, without both our families being deeply hurt and maybe broken. But be very clear that I do not feel guilt about what we were to each other—guilt only that I felt I had to end it. At that time, I wrote to you 'One cannot always be torn in two.' I remember the words because there were tears in my eyes as I wrote them—and are now again as I write this. I wish you could put your hands on my head in your lap, as I remember you doing so clearly. Forgive me, my dear love. I should at least have contacted you long ago.

Chittacobra? Well, here is the story. Something in my heart told me I had to find you again, so I googled your name. Thank God you are famous. Among the references I found two interviews you had done—one talking about your writings in which you outlined *Chittacobra* and the trees along the barren road, and one on Delhi, in which you spoke of the effect of evening light on the two lovers of *Chittacobra*. What you said set my heart racing.

First, I wrote to the only address I could find (on the Jain Samaj website, which incidentally has a photo of you just as I remember you) but they seemed to have the wrong address and my letter seemed to vanish. Finally, I emailed the lady who forwarded my email address to you—and you know the rest. I don't know why, but I was determined to find you again—so we have even more reasons to thank the wonders of modern technology.

It was only during this process that I tracked down a copy of *The Colour of my Being* in a bookshop in London. I bought it, only to find that some thirty pages were missing. I went back and got another complete copy from them, and also one of *Chittacobra* and *Kathgulab* from another Indian bookshop in London. (I have yet to track down *Daffodils on Fire* but I will, I will).

So you see, my Maya, that it was the need to contact you that led me to *Chittacobra*, not the other way round!

Enough for now—even the memories are exhausting.

Your K

M@chaurasta.com to K
18 July 2008

Yes my dearest love, memories are exhausting. I seem to find scant energy for anything else these days. I have no bad memories connected with you. Surprisingly none at all.

The demons are in my own head. Things, events, which seemed routine when they happened during the time we spent together; things not connected with you, just coincidental, grew so painful over time that I blocked them out. Now, when I recall that time, they break into my deliberate forgetfulness and breach the carefully built facade of strength. I can reason them into insignificance but they take their toll.

I understand and empathize with what you say about not causing pain to the loved ones. But for me marriage vows have meant nothing at all. That is my personal view and has nothing to do with religion, faith or anything else.

I would not have opted out, of course, but that was because of the children, and also my husband and I were comfortable with each other till the tragedy happened...I have no regrets about having loved, none at all.

I did want to know what came first, the egg or the chicken, *Chittacobra* or your desire to contact me. Don't know why. Thanks for answering my question.

Maya

K@crossroads.com to M
Jul 18, 2008

Maya, Maya

You said at the start of this reunion that I had come just at the right time. Certainly I have no idea why you so suddenly came back to my mind and heart, and I had to find you again. Something must have been calling me over the years and miles.

I understand your feeling about marriage vows. I remain, honestly, a Christian, and therefore have to believe that marriage vows are sacred. Yet, I feel no guilt but only deep gratitude and love about our relationship.

Love,

K

M@chaurasta.com to K
19 July 2008

I am so glad to have the lovely memories of us together being brought back. I am doubly glad and grateful to know that there is someone out there who loves me still and with whom I can share my feelings.

I can of course write you superficial happy romantic letters as if nothing was amiss, but that won't be me. The price of loving me is to occasionally peer into the deep ravine of my negation. In a way it helps that I do not have to face you when I write this; in another way it is so much easier to speak, because one can leave a lot unsaid, than put it in black and white.

You know, my love, excessive grief is highly embarrassing. It shows on one's face, making people uncomfortable. They don't know what to do, so instead of just sitting quietly and leaving after a while, they feel compelled to give advice. They tell me to read Gita or Gurbani or Qoran or Bible or whatever comes first to mind. They leave religious booklets or tomes of their faiths behind.

As if I hadn't read Gita before! Did I not know that Sri Krishna, who so calmly told Arjun not to feel guilty about killing his elders in the battle because they were, for all practical purposes dead, was struck dumb when Arjun's young son was killed by devious means? If philosophy deserted God himself, what possible solace could it give me? That one question was enough to make them disappear from my sight, for a while— but they were pig-headed enough to return with the same sermons.

There were exceptions, like my son's friends, who came and demanded food as they used to earlier; who said they came because they enjoyed being with me and loved talking about my son; that they never felt he was not there. They also took away the booklets, brochures and tomes to allow me to breathe. But they were young, with a future before them, so gradually they went away.

I then buried my memories deep within me and got on with enacting the sham of living. Gradually I guess life claimed me again. But the memories! It is not just the time spent with you. Anything can trigger a spate of painful memories, which make me believe that my whole life was a preparation for that one tragedy.

You know, right from childhood, even before I was married, I suffered from the irrational but intense fear that my child will die while I was away from him. When I had children, I was afraid of leaving them for long, though I kept telling myself that I was an utter fool to indulge in such irrationality.

Each time a child fell ill or hurt itself in my absence, which perversely they did, my fear was renewed. As I remembered Bombay, I also remembered how my four-year-old son had fallen and broken his arm and was taken to the hospital by someone in my absence when I was with you.

It had nothing to do with you. Such things were forever happening and I did not sit at home all the time. But each time anything like that happened, I was overly distraught but also told myself that my fear was balderdash.

Gradually I rid myself of it and built the opposite equally irrational faith that whatever else may happen in my life, nothing could happen to my sons as long as I was alive.

The children were grown, married men by then, and I was away in order to write! And then the nightmare came true.

Now...anything can trigger a memory of some small lapse and I relive the nightmare. The scent of tuberoses, a red flower, the smell of cooking, the wail of the shehnai...anything and I am back in the abyss.

This is getting inordinately long. I don't want to frighten you away. Promise me, love, never to feel guilt where I am concerned, otherwise I will be forced to resort to playacting with you too. I promise to face up to my fears and perhaps not talk about them. You shall certainly have a more congenial me next time.

Maya

K@crossroads.com to M
Jul 19, 2008

Dearest Maya,

Of course you must be yourself, especially with me—and nothing you could say would turn me away from you.

Certainly I have no advice to offer you—only that I am here
to share to any extent I can. I'll happily pay what you call the
price of loving you.

You must be yourself, but surely that self is not composed only
of pain and regret. Somewhere there must still be happiness
and even laughter. Maybe I have little to offer you, since my
life has obviously been almost completely free of the kind
of sorrow you know—and my memories of you, a total and
unmitigated joy. I see you in them now, smiling and laughing,
and I cannot believe those have gone forever!

With my love,

K

M@chaurasta.com to K
20 July 2008

No, it is not gone forever, my dearest love, there is happiness
and laughter, often enough. There are days, weeks when I am
quite like my old self, then like an alcoholic backsliding, I fall
in this black mood.

You asked me in one of your letters if marriage had helped. No,
it did not. For the simple reason that the same event means
totally different things to different people. My husband had
lost a son too and we started to plant the small forest together
at the site of the accident. But our aims were different.

I wanted to build a small cottage in the midst of the trees
and stay there by myself till I had come to terms with things.
He wanted to do charity to assuage his guilt at using our
daughter-in-law to persuade our son to go to Alwar to look
after his factory there. They were so young and so used to
hectic city life that they drove to Delhi at all odd hours on
a notoriously accident-prone road. I lived in fear all the time

they were there; only four months. They had shifted there while I was in Europe. Then what I had feared happened!

The charity lasted five years. Meanwhile he, who is a gambler by nature, had taken to investing in more and more risky enterprises till he went bankrupt. He had convinced himself that he was doing it to finance the clinic because I wanted it. No amount of my telling him that I did not made any difference!

Fortunately, after five years, just as the money disappeared, WHO, the authority which regulates how free TB medicine is to be distributed, decided that govt. emissaries would go to the patients' doorstep, so we could close the clinic. So, none of the patients suffered. I suppose God has small salves to offer for big wounds. The ultimate wrench came when, after holding out for three years, I finally had to let the govt. acquire the memorial land to pay back my husband's debts.

So, two years ago, I lost the memorial too. You know, I have a theory that everyone loses what he cherishes most in life. I have the fortunes of the characters in the Mahabharata to support me. Who am I then to be spared the grand irony?

I am sorry to use you again as my shrink. But I felt your presence so intensely beside me the whole of last night that I thought, let me share this too with you and be done! One thing I am sure of now, I do love you! And as well as ever I did.

K@crossroads.com to M
Jul 21, 2008

Dear dear Maya,

Your story leaves me both moved and aching for you. It explains so much in your previous emails that I could not fully understand. If you felt my presence with you last night, maybe I am helping in some small way.

Are you carrying the whole burden alone?

More later—for now, just love,

Kevin

M@chaurasta.com to K
21 July 2008

No. My son Ashwin and his wife are a great support. We have a fun relationship. She keeps gifting me young-looking Western clothes and accessories in fashion. Western clothes I wear mostly when I am in Bangalore or abroad, but accessories I use all the time. So life is not at all bad. When I am in Bangalore we have loads of fun.

I don't much care for Delhi now as a city to live in, but for a Hindi writer, living in Bangalore is like living in a foreign country. Though I have lot of friends there and I interact with those writing in English, it is not the same. It also does not have the vibrancy of Delhi. Maybe I'm better off in Delhi, fighting with all and sundry. Better to be annoyed than bored! Any day.

Remember Chekov's three sisters hankering for Moscow! We are three writer sisters but I guess I am the worst hankerer of the three!

To recompense you for my whining let me send you a sweet little story. You will enjoy reading it, I'm sure. With lots of love,

Maya

The Boy

I

At school

My son was in fourth grade at school. The teacher was droning on and on in the history class. Suddenly she swooped on him.

'Name Akbar's father,' she said.

'I don't know,' he replied.

'Why? Were you not listening to what I was saying?'

'No.'

'Why not?'

'I was thinking.'

'What about?'

'Just thinking.'

'Indeed. So what were you thinking?'

'If I knew that, I would have stopped thinking, wouldn't I?'

Was the teacher angry!

'You are inattentive and rude. Come with me to the Principal. I am reporting you.'

The Principal was in a quandary. Was it wrong to think? Wrong to be truthful, he pondered laboriously. What was wrong and what was right? What was more important, to think and search for the truth or to listen to a recital of facts?

The teacher was listing her complaints in great detail and suggesting retribution of various kinds. She went on and on, then stopped to ask, 'So, what is your answer?'

'Sorry', he said, 'I didn't hear you.'

'I said, what's your answer?'

'Not that. I didn't hear what you said earlier.'

'None of it! How? Why?'

'I was thinking.'

'What were you thinking?'

''If I knew that... he began then stopped. He was getting corrupted!

Duty first. The boy was suspended with a warning. If he did that sort of thing again, he could face expulsion.

Soon after that, the Principal resigned without anyone asking him to.

II

Shoes

The boy passed the tenth grade exam, not exactly with flying colours but well enough. Better than his teacher predicted and worse than we, the parents expected. I, his mother, blamed the below par performance on the attack of jaundice he had a couple of months before the exam. His teacher believed it was his cussed obstinacy, which made him do better than she expected.

He had also passed the written test for the Junior Talent Scholarship and was to appear for the viva voce the next day. Suddenly he developed high fever. No matter, I thought, it would go down by next morning thanks to modern medicine.

A clean and well-pressed pair of shirt and trousers hung in the closet in preparation for the interview. But the shoes still needed a coat of polish.

It was evening. The fever remained quite high. The shoes lay unpolished.

'Why not send them to the cobbler to be polished since you are not well enough to do it yourself,' I suggested.

'No,' he said,' I'll do it.'

'When?'

No answer.

'You have to leave early. There won't be time in the morning.'
Silence.

Perhaps he had fallen asleep. Let him rest.

I waited for an hour or so then sat down to a good scrub and polish. I enjoyed the shoes coming alive under my hands. One moment they were a pair of filthy street urchins; the next, well-clad, well-scrubbed public school denizens. Good. There was nothing like polishing shoes to see the mirror image of one's true face and loving heart. I felt quite proud of myself. I put them beside his bed. He would see them first thing in the morning.

He did.

I took his temperature. Still high. Never mind. He would cope. I made breakfast, put it on the table and went back to his room to call him.

He sat on the floor with the shoes in his hands.

'I polished them last night,' I said.

'I know,' he said and picked up the brush.

I could not help notice the condition the shoes were in; practically coated with mud. Apparently he had taken some of it off with the help of the cloth which lay on the floor. Now was the turn of the brush, which he held poised in his hand.

'But how...' I spluttered.

'I brought the mud from the garden to put on them. No one polishes my shoes but me.'

III

It Was Big

The boy, now a man of twenty, was working in San Francisco when the great earthquake hit the city. So I heard, read and saw on TV. All telephone lines were down, so there was no way I could contact him for the next two days.

I sat glued to the television, watching the same scenes of disaster played over and over again

I finally managed to talk to him on the phone after thirty-six anxious hours.

'Are you alright?' I asked breathlessly.

'The cup broke,' he said.

'Your friends...they are safe?'

'Yes-yes but...'

'The people at your office, Joe, his family, are they alright?'

'Guess so. The cup broke.'

What goddamn cup was he talking about!

Aloud I said, 'Was it very precious?'

'No. It was in the center of the empty table and it broke.'

'You saw it break?'

'Yes. I had just put it back in the middle of the dining table. There was nothing else there. Yet it broke. You understand?'

'I do,' I said, 'the quake was real bad.'

'It was not bad,' he said, 'It was big.'

K@crossroads.com to M
Jul 21, 2008

Dear one,

Thanks for the lovely little story. Thank God you have not lost your sense of humour and your deft touch in writing. Also good to know that you do have love and support. When do you go off to Bangalore and for how long?

You say you wear Western clothes sometimes in Bangalore or abroad. That brings back one very intense memory. I only remember ever seeing you in a dress rather than a sari just once—but an unforgettable once. I think I was staying in Delhi in a hotel possibly called Broadway, and you came to me in a long flowing dress—and I also remember even more vividly what happened to the dress and to us. You were breathtaking and wonderful. I assume you still are! Like you, I do not feel like a senior and I certainly intend to go on growing older disgracefully!

Have had a busy day, and just got to the computer, so am writing this at 5.30 p.m. here—you must be just about going to bed.

Sleep well, my love,

Kevin

M@chaurasta.com to K
22 July 2008

Dear One,

Did I really mostly wear a sari when I met you? I would have thought I would have worn salwar-kurta more than a sari. I remember changing from a short top to a longer one to go to Gandhi Darshan in Delhi, and you saying 'how does a few more inches of cloth show more respect?' Memory is so strange; it brings back such snippets suddenly. Now did I imagine it or did it really happen?

I do remember the long dress. Sunshine yellow it was. We went to see Indrani Rahman's dance recital later. Weren't they the early days of our meeting? Was I still in Durgapur? I can't recall.

You do seem to remember a lot. They say women remember things, men don't. You certainly prove that wrong.

I leave for Bangalore on 3rd August. There's time still. Today was a hectic day. It's now around ten at night. Good night for now.

Love,

Maya

`K@crossroads.com to M`
`Jul 22, 2008`

Yes my love, you are right. It was often the salwar-kurta—
and sometimes a sari, but only once, the dress! Yes indeed
it was sunshine yellow, and seemed to echo the bright joy of
being with you that day. I do not know if you were still in
Durgapur... Probably not, since why then would we need to
meet in Delhi?

May it not be that women and men remember in different
ways? You remember many of the places we went to in more
detail, and some of the things I said to you at different times.
Certainly Richard seemed to be saying eccentric things!

For me, the intense memories are of the many times we were
fully together, and I do believe I remember them all. Maybe
you don't want that kind of remembering, but I could tell you
step by step all that happened the day of the yellow dress—and
on many other occasions. Test me on my memories sometime.

Meanwhile you will be off to bed again! Sleep well, beloved.

Kevin

`M@chaurasta.com to K`
`23 July 2008`

Dearest,

I remember the places because they are familiar to me. I pass
by all the time. I don't remember the name of the hotel or
anything about the street or place, the only time we met in
London. Maybe if you pass that hotel, whatever its name,
you'll remember more about the environs.

I remember Indrani Rahman's dance recital because of an
interesting aside. Apparently my father was there in the hall

with two premium passes. He knew I was going there so wanted to give them to me. He looked around but could not see me. Was he taken aback when I returned! Very chivalrously, he said, I did see a lovely young lady in a sunset dress but did not realize it was you.

See what I mean.

My dear sister insisted I had never gone there! Was off God knows where.

When I pass Sapru House, close to my father's house, where the recital took place, I remember not only you but my father, my sister, my first book release there with Jainendra as the Chair. Also, a psychopathic but genius author, who used to stalk me and chose to heap highbrow praise on my book. All gone now, except you. But you were as good as gone till your revival.

It is also partly the bane of being a writer. In the beginning when I wrote my stories, they kept saying, geography, dear, geography! Why have your tales no geography? I guess as one continues writing it comes naturally.

I don't mind your reminding me of the memories you have. Not that I don't have them. But let me see if in your recital, I recognize the hare-brained young woman as me or feel removed from her? You know what's most thrilling? To be sitting at the computer and have the inbox flash a mail, which happens to be yours! So far it has happened only once.

To your memories and mine,

Maya

K@crossroads.com to M
Jul 23, 2008

Maya Maya,

Your name trips off my tongue and warms me as I say it.

The hotel in London was the Strand Palace in the Strand. I have often passed it since and always with memories of you. We sat in the lobby talking to each other—kind of fencing to see if the old magic was still there—and I think later we proved it was—different yet the same. It is good to know that you too feel something when you pass by places we shared.

Loved your story of the dance recital—you must have had a very understanding and gracious father! I can so easily picture 'a lovely young lady in a sunset dress' though I would have called it sunrise!

Was it the same sister I met once? Seemed to be quite understanding of at least a romantic friendship, if not more!

As for the hare-brained young woman, well, you once wrote to me as 'the old crazy', so I suppose neither of us was immune from a touch of madness. But for me it has lasted, and I refuse to believe that you are not still, in some real sense, my Maya.

I once wrote to you in a train going back to Calcutta, with fresh memories of you in my heart, words that I think I can quote virtually exactly. I wrote 'the love marks on my body will fade soon enough, but the love marks on my soul will last forever.' They were true.

Love,

K

`K@crossroads.com to M`
`Jul 25, 2008`

Nothing special. Just to say I am thinking of you. Love, K

`M@chaurasta.com to K`
`26 July 2008`

Computer has conked off. Will write later

`M@chaurasta.com to K`
`31 July 2008`

Dearest,

At last, I have installed a new computer!

Your question about my sister triggered a whole lot of memories about my sisters. The sister who questioned my Sapru House sojourn was my elder sister, the one my novel is about. The one you met briefly once was my kid sister, who has since married and turned into a writer. So now we are a family with three writer sisters. Something odd about the family, I can hear you say under your breath. You are quite right my love. Shades of Bronte! We even boast of a Barnwell Bronte.

But now, of the sister you did not meet. Elder to me by two years, she was a famous writer, in every way my opposite—world view, outlook on life and of course, writing style. She was the traditionalist, I the rebel.

Yet the irony is that it was she who fell in love with an out of caste, non-brilliant, work-shy and wastrel son of opulent parents with no plan for caring for others, or himself for that matter. He did have oodles of charm and an encyclopaedic knowledge of trivia, but all he had in the name of aspiration or ambition was this prodigious romantic passion. My sister

Madhavi gave up her studies, magnificent suitors and brilliant career for love and married him. But that did not prevent her from forever lecturing me against rebellion or love marriages for that matter, as they were then called in India, or breaking well-honed customs. In fact while she was at her asexual rendezvous with her boy-friend, she was so terrified of being discovered by our numerous relatives and well-wishers in Delhi that she always took me along. As a result, the boys at the university thought I had a steady boyfriend, who stalked me with roses, chocolates, notes and whatnot in a flaming red sports car; little knowing that the goodies were for my sister; that I was a mere go-between, like the friend in classical plays. All prospects of a love life for me were effectively wrecked, but I had loads of fun with him. We became friends, so I was taken to plays, fetes, cafes, parks; everywhere my sister was afraid to be seen with him. Surprisingly it never occurred to her to be jealous of me.

Despite our almost total disagreement on larger issues, we sisters remained close, ever-squabbling friends with no secrets. When she read *Chittacobra*, her immediate remark was, 'Whom are you kidding...no one writes like that without first-hand experience!' She then went on to lecture me on the pitfalls of extra-marital affairs, citing Madame Bovary, Anna Karenina, et al. After all she almost had a Masters in English literature, had always topped the class in Delhi University, but squandered the actual degree by bunking the last exam. Her boyfriend had failed all of them and she did not want him to feel bad!

But when the push came to shove and I was threatened with arrest she stood by me, despite unending advice to expunge the offending remarks and be done with it. On an impulse, one Friday we decided to go meet the Lt. Governor and persuade him to withdraw the complaint. So we went—dressed to kill—to Raj Bhawan, way out in North Delhi in a DTC bus if you please. Guess my husband must have taken the solitary car between us to office. Throughout the hour-long journey, she never stopped chiding me for writing the way I did. 'At this rate Ishara will be making films on your stories soon,' she declared, much to the amusement of the bus passengers. Ishara was notorious for making sexually explicit Hindi films in the '80s. I pretended not to hear, to ward off further diatribe, and we got down at the Old Secretariat bus stop in cagey silence.

Madhavi imperiously asked the prim and proper military guard at the gate, 'How far is Raj Bhawan from here?'

'Just two steps,' he replied.

'Yours or mine?' she enquired innocuously. He took one look at her Marilyn Monroe figure and giggled like a smitten adolescent. That melted the chill between us and we went laughing the rest of the way.

Once at the Guv House, the conversation went something like this: —We want to meet the Governor. —Do you have an appointment? —No we don't, that's why we have come to you. —Ok, I can get you an appointment with his PS for Monday. —No-no, we need to see the Governor now...we are desperate and have come from so far. —Where? —Safdarjung Development Area (South Delhi). —SDA, he snorted, that's not far, I live there. —Fine, my sister pounced on him. Then be a good neighbour (*tab aap padosi dharm nibhaiye*, is what she said in Hindi, making good neighbourliness into a dharma or pious act.)

Something about us must have appealed to his sense of humour because he said, would after lunch do? Absolutely, I gushed, but could we have some tea, she is very diabetic. She was, mortally diabetic, died of it at the age of 62. But that came sixteen years later. The idea of a sexy diabetic collapsing in the Guv office must have rattled him, because he sent in tea with loads of biscuits, which we had to eat to keep up the pretence of imminent collapse. Madhavi ate and scolded at the same time for my bringing up her diabetes and denting her erotic image.

Soon, we were in the presence of Lt. Governor Khurana in post-lunch langour—his not ours. He heard us perfunctorily and assured us that the Delhi Administration had no business to harass a writer for a novel however bold (euphemism for obscene) and the order would be revoked. We thanked him profusely as we got up to go.

'Where are you going', he woke up to call out, 'Give the book to me!' I handed it to him while my sister leaned over and whispered, 'Will your heart stand it!'

Later when the order remained unrevoked I accused her of alienating the Guv with that sentence, but I knew it was because the Guv himself had got booted out with a change in government. A year later the new one finally rescued me, as you know from my essay.

More about her some other time.

Love,

M

K@crossroads.com to M
Jul 31, 2008

Maya,

Welcome back. It is incredible after more than thirty years, but I missed you. Thank god for whoever invented the internet!

What a scintillating story about your sister and you. Some vigour your charming sister and you had, and such a complex vibrant relationship.

Yes, tell me more when you feel like.

K

M@chaurasta.com to K
5 August 2008

Dearest,

This last week with the bomb blasts all over the country, including the safe haven of Bangalore, has driven all pleasant thoughts from my mind. Now it is time to go there. I'll write from there.

M

K@crossroads.com to M
Aug 5, 2008

Maya,

Yes, the news of the bombs pained me too. I must admit to having a strong prejudice, a conviction that the Partition of India and the creation of Pakistan was a colossal mistake, which has led in the end to much of what we now see.

Lord Mountbatten is on record as saying that he tried to avert the tragedy, and held out against Jinnah as long as he could. He said, had he known how ill Jinnah was, and how soon his life would end, he would have held out, and he believed that nobody else in the League, would have resisted an undivided country.

Ah well, we cannot change history, good or bad.

Hope all goes well with you in Bangalore.

Love,

K

M@chaurasta.com to K
5 August 2008

My dear Kevin,

The creation of Pakistan was as much the doing of Lord Mounbatten and Nehru as Jinnah. It was Jinnah who was willing to wait. That is the grand irony. It was the other two who wanted things done in a hurry to get maximum credit. Nehru was not willing to give up being Prime Minister, and Mountbatten wanted things done so he could get the credit for India's Independence. The colossal egos of three misguided men have left us with this mess. That is the name of the game called history where the ordinary people always lose.

Anyway, we can only hope the darkness will be followed by light.

Love,

M

K@crossroads.com to M
Aug 5, 2008

Dearest Maya,

The last thing I want is to get into a political discussion with you—not unless we could do it face to face!

My facts may be mistaken, but I do not believe that Mountbatten's life-long regret and deep sorrow at what he believed he had been compelled to do, was not genuine. My understanding comes from the book *Freedom at Midnight*, which records the meetings held and their outcome.

Anyway, no more of this. Keep me posted on what you feel about things, including your own life—and whether Bangalore brings you some happiness. It feels good to be in touch with you again—even if we begin with an argument!

With my love,

the old crazy

M@chaurasta.com to K
6 August 2008

Dearest,

I cannot let this go unanswered. *Freedom at Midnight* is the most undependable book I have ever read. Any book which is so one-sided and clichéd has to be. I am surprised that you, who fought for an autonomous Scottish Parliament should be taken in by somebody so like Margaret Thatcher as Mountbatten. My new novel obliquely touches on the perversity of so called eye-witnesses.

I see no harm in a political discussion among thinking people. My individual life is mixed up with the larger issues. But if you say so, definitely no more of this.

Love,

Maya

`K@Crossroads.com to M`
`Aug 7, 2008`

Maya, Maya,

OK, I stand corrected. I think I would find your anger very attractive! By all means let us go further into this, though I do wish I could actually talk to you about this, and many things. Do tell me more both about your criticisms of *Freedom at Midnight*, and about the reasons and grounds for your criticism of both Nehru and Mountbatten. I read the book long ago. If Mountbatten was anything like Maggie Thatcher, I would indeed be appalled (is that how you spell it?) if he took me in! Anyhow, my view of the mistake of Partition remains firm!

I suppose my reluctance was not that I did not want to discuss these issues with you, certainly not that I do not deeply respect your intelligence and views. It was just that I did not want anything to damage the love between us—but that was foolish I know.

How does your novel touch on the perversity of eyewitnesses?

In that vein, your poems brought tears to my eyes. As you know better than anyone, despite the air of confidence and rationality I show to most people, I can be very emotional and vulnerable. Maybe I fell on my head when I was a baby!

Love,

Kevin

`M@chaurasta.com to K`
`7 August 2008`

You sure did. But bye and love for now. More from Bengalaru.
M

M@chaurasta.com to K
8 August 2008

Here I am in Bengaluru and naturally Mountbatten, Nehru and all unsavoury topics have gone clean out of my head. Anyway, it is a long story, and longer still when you try to explain it to someone who has never been part of the Indian struggle.

I thought the Mountbatten myth had been exploded even in Britain with the newer biographies coming out. As far as India is concerned, no one was taken in by him except Nehru. But they were two of a kind in the exaggerated notions of their greatness. Both liked to play minor monarchs, which Mountbatten could as Viceroy and later thanks to Nehru, as Governor General.

Nehru fancied himself as a great world leader and placed his personal image and reputation above what was best for the country. I have that as part of the background of my new novel *Miljul Mann*. Declaring a ceasefire and going to the UN, when the Indian army was within an inch of pushing out the aggressors out of Kashmir, against the express admonition of Sardar Patel, to win brownie points from the world is one example. The resulting partition of J&K has had, as everyone knows, more disastrous consequences on terrorism than the Partition of India. Of course, the English Governer General backed Nehru fully!

In fact if Mountbatten & co—who preponed the proposed date of India's Independence and made the final draft about the Princely States much too hastily, without due preparation, and in a wholly uncaring way—had had their way, India would have been balkanized and found itself divided into perhaps more than ten nations. Only Sardar Patel and his strategy stood in their way and he did manage to cobble a nation together. He failed to hold Nehru on Kashmir and disaster followed.

There is too much to say on this. I will have to write a whole treatise to clarify things, but to put it succinctly:

1. Gandhi suggested that the Congress be disbanded and a new political party formed after Independence. Earlier he had suggested that Jinnah could be first PM of undivided India (Nehru could wait his turn) as a move to prevent Partition. No way! Nehru would never agree to that! Nehru was Gandhi's pet, but by 1947 even he was disenchanted with him. For once he wanted him to give up the number one position.

2. To quote my father who was part of the Gandhi-Nehru brigade. 'None of them have any idea of governance. They should all continue in Class A jails after Independence, where they should be encouraged to talk philosophy and write books. Choose other leaders to govern the country.'

My novel *Anitya* is at last being translated in English. Maybe someday you could read it and get an idea of what happens to a nation forced to live in a state of perpetual dilemma, created by an artificial barrier between non-violent and violent freedom movements.

Freedom at Midnight is written wholly from the viewpoint of Mountbatten's utterances and the popular Nehruvian myth. Or shall we say cliché. Enough of politics!

But politics does not interfere with love, dear.

M

K@crossroads.com to M
Aug 8, 2008

Dearest Maya,

Thank you. The passion that breathes through your email leaves me breathless. My only dear wish is that I could at least hear you telling me these things, hear the passion in your voice.

I accept that because of who and what I am, I may never, as you say, understand something that can only be fully understood by those who shared in the real struggle. Scotland's battle to be a nation cannot be compared with that of India, I accept. But I could speak about it, and have spoken and written about it, with something approaching your fire!

Yes, you are as always, right about us. Politics indeed does not interfere with love—but it does have a relationship. It changes, maybe even deepens love.

Love,

K

M@chaurasta.com to K
9 August 2008

Dearest,

Of course you have! I have it on record. Scotland's battle for Independence might not have been on as gigantic a scale as India's but it needed no less passion and commitment. And, after all, it changed your life as well as Scotland's. You became a politician and negotiator par excellence and retired as a clergyman.

But my passion has got me in trouble throughout my life. I am all kinds of a fool. Whenever there is somebody who can be of help to me in my career, I manage to quarrel with him on some matter of pure principle and scuttle my prospects. Keki Daruwalla asked me once, 'how did you manage to fall foul of both the male and female counterpart of the literary establishment? To lose one could be a misfortune, but to quote Oscar Wilde, "to lose both smacks of carelessness."'

You are different. I am in no danger of losing your love and fortunately, you cannot be of use to me in any material way. But even if things were different, I am no good at dissimulation. I'm sure that's not the correct spelling. But no matter.

About my new novel...it tells the story of two sisters, told by one sister and a writer. Their versions, though both were eyewitnesses, are as different from each other as were the records of India's Independence Movements.

My love, I am quite at ease with disagreement about political beliefs and ideas in general but I reserve the right to be not convinced. It does not sour personal relationships. Come to think of it, I could have fallen in love with Nehru but alas, I was only nine years old!

I'll send you my essay on 'My World My Writing' called 'No Amulets Against Lust'. It is rollicking fun.

With all my love,

M

No Amulets Against Lust

When you ask a writer to talk about her world, it is bound to be partly fiction. No matter. After all, things are never what they seem, so one's world may be fiction and fiction, a chronicle of facts. In any case, the moment you experience a fact, it turns into fiction.

It's the same with the positives and negatives in life. So it's not strange that when I try to separate the positive inputs of my life from the stumbling blocks, I find they are in fact the same. For example, I used to be a sickly child. That meant missing school, games and the opportunities to make friends. But it had a positive side as it propelled me from action to reflection. It was a short step to literature, first reading then writing. Thanks to my father, who thought that anyone on the brink of death would want to read the great masters, I read Tolstoy, Dostoevsky, Chekhov, Henry James, Shakespeare, Jainendra, Rabindranath Thakur, at an early age. But they were not the only ones. I gave myself a fair dose of popular writers like Maugham, Oscar Wilde, Graham Greene, P.G. Wodehouse, Jane Austen et al.

Reading the masters took my mind off my illness. Not going to school for three years helped me concentrate on 'out of course' books. Interestingly, Manohar Shyam Joshi called all non-conformist writing, 'out of course.' It also made me lose fear of eminence. I could look the most famous man in the eye and discuss his work fearlessly. How powerful a stumbling block candour was to material progress, I discovered later. So much later that it was too late to change my attitude.

An undisputed positive input in my life was the fact that, as a child, I never knew that girls were supposed to behave differently from boys. That they were supposed to have a different education or ambition or mindset. The credit goes to my father, who never bemoaned having five daughters in a row. Nor did he enlighten us about exclusively feminine virtues or accomplishments. We were expected to educate ourselves and get on with our lives. Marriage was neither inevitable nor an anathema.

My mother's influence was more subtle. She was neither a career woman nor a good housekeeper or mother, not even passable. She did not like children, though she had six of them for my father to bring up. She possessed the remarkable quality of absolute honesty and the capacity to keep secrets. She was the confidante of a host of writers and artists. She tendered advice on love matters from her bed, to which she was confined, being a chronic invalid. Surprisingly, this unusual state of affairs did not bother us. I was the least bothered of the siblings. We knew our mother was different and cherished her for it. Life in a house with no presiding mother figure was fraught with discomfort and irritants but it was never dull, predictable or stereotypical.

In the long run, this lack of maternal care turned into a positive input as it made me comfortable with non-stereotypical women. It had a great influence on my writing. When the orthodox males of the Hindi world told me that my women did not ring true as Bhartiya narees, I could ignore them, secure in the knowledge of the women of my family. There were others beside my mother, equally out of the box. There was a paternal great-grandmother, who prayed that her great daughter-in-law's first child be a girl. There was a maternal grandmother, who told her husband to fetch his friend to her, on her deathbed and went on to entrust the marriage of her only daughter to him, rather than her husband. She wanted her to marry a freedom fighter and her husband was a Cambridge-educated barrister.

Ironically, I married into a family that was down-to-earth, conformist, perfectly in sync with the societal dictates. The larger family's preoccupation with food helped me get over the mental block of not wanting to cook. Later, it earned me brownie points with not only my children but nieces and nephews. That was certainly a positive outcome. Also my intense loneliness in the midst of a large family helped me take to creative writing. It started as a refuge, but soon turned into a passion. It helped that none of my in-laws read me; I did not have to contend with Hindi critics within the family!

Challenge in any form is the propelling force of all creativity and I have had no dearth of it. Each bout of criticism and excommunication by male or male-dominated female writers and critics gave me fresh reasons to continue to write the only way I knew how.

I discovered when I started publishing my stories that the slightest deviation from the norm had the literary critics throwing up their hands and shrieking, Western sensibility! One of my earliest stories, 'Avkaash', published in Hindi in 1972 and soon after translated in English and German, a simple tale of an extra-marital affair, where the woman says all she wanted was a vacation and was glad to have had it, was the first to earn their ire. A mother of two and an affair, they said, impossible in Bharatvarsh! As if children are an amulet against lust! Lust, not love! It was the lack of hypocrisy, which angered them.

This thin-skinned stuff was not peculiar to the Hindi world. In 1991, Adil Jussawala, reviewing a collection of my stories, *Daffodils On Fire*, said, "Aversion, an understated story about a woman who has quietly gone mad and refuses to acknowledge the presence of her retired husband, is Maya Jain at her best." A classic case of killing with kindness! The protagonist was anything but mad. She was a poised householder who did not communicate with her husband because she did not want to. The Hindi critics could be excused for saying that they did not want my women to be their wives! Who wanted a woman, forever thinking, reasoning and looking deep inside you? Not an Indian male.

The strange thing was that when I did tell my own story, no one believed it. They commiserated with me saying, doesn't sound very plausible. After all it's a product of your imagination, not experience. My advice to all young people is, if you don't want them to know the truth about you, tell it all. Nobody believes the truth.

I am thankful that I am not a midnight's child. I have enough memories of the darker half of the night. My earliest memories are of the Quit India Movement of 1942. My novel, *Anitya,* came out of the dilemmas and dissentions that underlined our various Independence movements.

While researching and writing the novel, I realized that we are no worse human beings today than we were then. We might have been put to a harder test then, but the issue at stake was much simpler; getting rid of foreign rule. Domination is quite another matter. It can continue in subtle, complex and devious forms, as it does in our country, and is more difficult to fight. It is doubly difficult to be free in a free nation. Is it because the affluent world has gained a greater hold on us? Or having tasted the larger freedom, we expect everything else to follow? Are we content to indulge our freedom of expression, when we feel shackled, instead of struggling to break free? Freedom of choice is a hard taskmaster. It is not easy to be free but it sure is exhilarating.

The credo, which helped me weather many a storm was simple. When in doubt, I asked myself, what would I do if it were the last day of my life? It was an infallible way of separating the essential from the non-essential. It prevented me from getting swamped by societal injunctions. It also allowed me to see the funny side of adversity and injustice. Unfortunately, this worked only as long as there was a choice. When fate or chance took away all choices from me, when the last day of my life became irrelevant, I had to look for a brand-new credo. I then chose to fall back on satire. I knew if I could laugh at myself and at the powers, divine or otherwise, I could continue to write. I did.

Once you get used to exercising choice, you can sometimes create choices out of nothing. That is the lesson I have learnt from my confrontation with the real, the ethereal and the demonic world.

K@crossroads.com to M
Aug 10, 2008

Rollicking fun indeed, and so are you! And my love, whatever else you are, you are no kind of fool. You are what I, with typical male chauvinism, would call a very sharp cookie! To me, you are just Maya, and I am so glad to gradually come to know more of your life and vision. You have always been yourself—more honestly, I think than I have been, since I have essentially been the reconciler, the negotiator, the one who held the line and brought consensus, who always looked for compromise. That is indeed how we achieved the agreement that led to the Scottish Parliament. I irritated people, but carried on nevertheless.

With you at least I was not just honest, but truly myself. You once wrote of the lovers of *Chittacobra*, that 'they try to find their true personalities through their relationship.' I recognize the truth in that.

I have not yet had a chance to read your other article, 'Writing the Self', properly, but even from the first para, I can see the difference between my approach to the self, and yours. Maybe it is a male thing but I do think in chronological terms—even when I read *Chittacobra*, part of me wanted to know when each part was written or how they fit! I think it is part of the male tendency to blinkered vision and the female's greater ability to see always the periphery as well.

You know my attachment to Kierkegaard. I tend to look at my life in sectors, and of course, to interpret each in the light of events and outcomes. But I am blethering (good Scots word for rambling).

Thank God you were too young to fall in love with Nehru—though you might have changed the course of history, if you had!!

With my love,

K

M@chaurasta.com to K
10 August 2008

But dearest, I fully agree with Kierkegaard and you that life has to be understood backward. Without a sense of history, or what you call chronology, or an understanding of cause and effect, we will be but puppets to be danced at will by some dictator or leader (often unfortunately synonyms).

God knows and you do too, that I have made enough compromises in life for the love of children. Lots of young people come to me for advice and I am not bad at cobbling a compromise. What I cannot do is pretend that I believe in things to gain approval and awards.

Bhagat Singh said compromise is a good thing, an essential ingredient of negotiation, for keeping the door open. If you ask for 16 annas and get 8 you take them, and negotiate for more in future. But if you give away your right to ask for 16 annas and are ready to take whatever the other is willing to give, you get a fractured Independence like ours, with a fractured psyche.

Enough of philosophy. Bangalore has a lovely climate. It rains any time, like London. I mean that the rains are not concentrated in one dramatic phase of the monsoon but staggered through the year. It is so green that the saying goes, if you immerse your finger in the soil, it starts to grow. I am torn between spending my time outside or being cooped inside with my novel.

I have a lovely photograph of mine with Nehru when I was about twenty (1958), just after my graduation. At least I had. Can't find it now. One thing is indisputable. He was handsome and charming even then. No woman was totally immune. Unfortunately, just four years later came 1962 and the Indo-Chinese war, which brought Nehru's image crashing down. How's that for chronology!

It is a nice word, is blethering. Please do continue to blether.

M

K@crossroads.com to M
Aug 12, 2008

...

I had been having ectopic (irregular) beats for some time, and had a bad run in November 1990, when I was in Frankfurt airport waiting for a plane to Singapore, on my way to a church conference in Kota Kinabalu in Malaysia. I had time to go to the medical centre at the airport, where they did an ECG and said there was no immediate danger and I could continue my journey but that I should have an exercise ECG (treadmill) on my return.

This I did in February 1991 in Glasgow, and my cardiologist arranged an angiogram, which confirmed arterial heart disease, so bad that he recommended a triple by-pass.

By coincidence, the day I came home from the angiogram, I watched a TV programme about the claim of Dean Ornish in California, to reverse heart disease by a combination of strict diet, meditation and exercises. I found details of his programme, and told the surgeon I would not have invasive surgery but would try the Ornish method. That was twenty-four years ago! I had episodes of what turned out to be atrial fibrillation, but this was always put right either by medication or by shock. For years I followed the Ornish diet etc. faithfully, but gradually I have reverted to a normal diet and am still alive and kicking. My old cardiologist calls it a minor miracle!

I did have a second angiogram when I had the first episode of the atrial fibrillation in 2000—it showed no great difference. The amazing thing is that it has never stopped me doing anything, even in the most active periods of the last twenty years. When we last met, I must already have been on my new regime. Our meeting no doubt helped restore my zest for life, which is unabated—like yours I hope, despite everything.

...

M@chaurasta.com to K
13 August 2008

Dearest,

I feel quite alarmed at what you said in your truncated mail yesterday. As part of it was missing, I don't know how you got onto the topic of medical reports, but that doesn't matter. What alarmed me was what you said about your heart condition. I have to say that it's fine that the regimen has not prevented you from doing whatever you wanted to, even extreme activity, but 2000 was eight years ago. Should you not be having another angiogram?

Remember, dearest, that I am from India, where alternative medicine, including diet regimens, are the order of the day. But I also know from experience that a time may come you might have to resort to more conventional, rather modern medicine.

I am not a sceptic, nor do I want to send negative vibes, but why are you set against surgery? Anyway don't you think another angiogram should be done?

I can only add that in 2002, I exacerbated my illness by pretending it had gone away. I first fell ill in 2000. But when the drugs had rather virulent side effects, I settled for alternative treatment, without proper investigation. It meant that a decisive diagnosis was never made and I was free to pretend it was psychosomatic. So other combination drugs which could have helped were never tried. I felt well enough, but the outcome in 2002 was caused by that neglect.

That time I happened by chance to land in the OPD room of a famous lung specialist who, for some reason, took me on as a challenge. He was bent upon saving me from myself; his words. He put me in the ICU with the usual procedures, where trial with various drugs went on till he hit upon the right combo. I took it diligently for one year and was fully cured. I could travel to Suriname and Japan next year and also took on the job of writing the column in *India Today*. I am fine, thanks to that rather sentimental doctor.

This story is told not with a view to discourage you but just to say that sometimes it's not such a bad idea to get the tests done. But of course there are people whose clinical reports do not measure up to their own will to live or God's grace. So if you do not feel restricted, in effect you are not.

I know I sound utterly confused which I am. Sweetheart, do take care and write.

Love,

Maya

K@crossroads.com to M
Aug 13, 2008

Thanks my love. Don't worry about the angiograms. I have had repeated ECGs and echocardiograms over the years and always they show a normal heart. In general I feel absolutely well, alive and kicking, and you certainly have nothing to be alarmed about! Of course we are all mortal but I hope and intend to have a bit of time yet, as you do!

My previous cardiologist in Glasgow suggested that the heart has a way of finding new paths and constructing new filaments to bypass blockages, and that might be happening in my case. No, sorry darling, but I do not intend to keep having angiograms.

More important, three cheers for the sentimental lung specialist who managed to save you from yourself! Quite a job I would imagine!! You seem now to have recovered a will to live life to the full and to write. I am so glad that when I tried to find you on the internet, I was not told you had gone forever.

OK my love, that's it. I'm off in a few minutes to post the book to you.

K

P.S. Do read lines 24 and 25 of page 74. What they say is at best a half-truth. It's important to me that you know it.

M@chaurasta.com to K
14 August 2008

Dearest,

Yes the heart does have a way of getting around blockages both physically and otherwise, so I guess you will be good for quite a few more years.

Am looking forward to lines 24 and 25 on p. 74. My, does it sound like a Hardy boys mystery that my grandchildren read!

I had great hopes of the mysterious Kota Kinabalu. But Malaysia is just next door. Costs less to go there from Bangalore than to Delhi. I went to Malaysia in 2000 but only to KL and then to Langkawi, a nice little touristy island. It was a delightful place and I enjoyed it more than anything I had for a long time. Guess it was nice to see all the women as small built as I. All the lovely dresses seemed to fit me. No Kota Kinabalu for me. Alas, what a lovely sound!

Do you remember you once called patients of consumption 'interesting', while talking of opera divas? I recalled it often during my illness.

Also, when I got my essay on Delhi from *Tehelka*, I saw the accompanying photo of myself and realized I was at my plumpest when I met you in 1993, while you looked more trim and slim. I wondered if you had been unwell, then put it down to wanting to look young! And interesting!

I have lost around 10 kg since then and look quite 'interesting' now. I know I am talking utter nonsense but it's nice to let the mind loosen up.

Lots of love,

Maya

`K@crossroads.com to M`
`Aug 14, 2008`

Maya, Maya,

You used to call me the globe trotter—wondering where I was next. Well, you seem to be one, so much more than me now—living with a vengeance indeed!

Did I call patients of consumption interesting? That is one I don't remember. In what context did I say that?

I remember you in 1993 very clearly, but I do not remember you as 'at your plumpest'. That is not a word I would ever have thought of about you. I don't think I ever thought of you as small built either—just as one who fitted so naturally and wonderfully into my arms. Good to know you are interesting—never doubted it—but I still hope for an opportunity one day to find out how interesting.

Am I the one talking nonsense now? No, but even if we both are, keep talking!

With my love,

K

`M@chaurasta.com to K`
`18 August 2008`

Dearest,

Do you remember the trips you made to East Bengal when the War for Bangladesh was being fought? I remember you saying when you returned from East Bengal that it was probably the most horrifying month of your life. In fact, it got widely reported in the papers in UK. Then you said something which spoke to the writer in me.

'To think in millions is almost impossible. The tragedy becomes real to us only when we hear the individual stories...a man walking across the border carrying his 75-year-old crippled father. Or a woman sitting with two children on the roadside; the glazed faraway look of starvation on their faces. Beside her a shapeless bundle which was her dead infant. In our medical care unit, a man in his 70s had a strange wound—the tips of the fingers of his right hand had been shot off. I asked him how this had happened. He had seen other men of his village shot one by one and knelt with folded hands to plead for his life. The soldier had shot but missed any vital part.'

I think it was this that prompted me to write about Gangu, in *Chittacobra*, the traumatized deaf mute girl from Bangladesh whom Richard helped recover some balance as he taught her to make toys.

I envied you because I would have loved to go with you but never picked up enough courage. That's a kind of globetrotting I have never done.

Of course your mission in Calcutta provided aid that was customary. What made you the darling of the people and politicians was that you spoke Bangla so fluently! The invitation to the Govt House in Dhaka by President Syed Choudhery in 1974 came because you spoke in both Bangla and English, at the Trafalgar Square meeting, not because your words were, oh so wise! You know!

How come you have forgotten Bangla? Lack of practice I suppose.

It was galling for me that you two Brits would break into Bangla in Durgapur so we, non-Bengalis could not understand you. I vowed to learn Bangla and read out portions of Tagore's *Shesher Kabita* to you. And I did. Do you remember? I'm sure you don't. How can you when I have forgotten whatever

Bangla I had and you say you have little of it now. But I had just learnt it to settle a score. You should not have forgotten any of your Bangla because you were so fluent in it; but then you say you can sing the Russian National anthem without understanding a word of Russian. Some Krazy I fell in love with.

And I never knew where your next letter would be from; Istanbul, Copenhagen or Congo! Or where you would suddenly fly out to Delhi from! I remember you coming in once in a plane delivering mail from some remote land and reaching Delhi at the crack of dawn. Was I startled awake by your voice on the phone! No such adventures for me.

When I said plumpest, I guess I meant least thin. Slim if you want to be polite. You know I have always wanted to put on some weight and be a little plump. The closest I came being, living life to the full happy plump, was in early 1993. When I met you, I was at the peak of everything in my life, health, career, happiness. It was downhill after that, till I laboriously trudged up and gained some height. But not weight. The photo was actually taken in Berlin just before I came to London.

We were talking of operas and classics, where the diva or heroine was almost always consumptive and dying as in that Henry James novel... *Mellissa*? In *The Portrait of a Lady*, it was the man who was consumptive. Someone had to be to make it...you guessed it, interesting.

I have to go now. Will continue later,

M

K@crossroads.com to M
Aug 18, 2008

No man is a hero to his valet or astute lover, and who more astute than you. So I will not quibble with your remarks about my wowing them with my Bangla! But it was not all flummery, I really cared about Bangladesh, you know that. I have the President of Bangladesh on record acknowledging my contribution (!) to the making of Bangladesh.

But you have scant respect for Presidents or Prime Ministers, so we'll let that pass.

But dearest, you are wrong about my not remembering you reciting *Shesher Kabita* to me. With my photographic memory for poetry, I can quote the last poignant verse to you; but in plebeian English.

Do not mourn for me,
You have your work, I have my world.
My vessel has not become empty
To fill it is my mission.
Whatever I gave you
It is now your absolute possession.
What I have to give now
Are the hourly offerings from my heart.
You are incomparable, you are rich!
Whatever I gave you
It was but your gift
You made me so much indebted
As much as you took.
My friend, farewell!

I can still savour on my tongue the passionate lilt in your voice as you said *Hey bondhu bidai* in Bangla and see the mischief in your eye. I thought you might be making fun of Tagore. What a fitting blow to my vanity; you were settling a score. But my love, the passion was undoubtedly for me or rather us! Right now, bondhu, all I wish for is that I could startle you out of sleep!

Waiting for the opportunity bondhu, bidai!

K

M@chaurasta.com to K
18 August 2008

Kevin my dear Love,

I am back. It is 9.30 at night. It is raining hard. Not cats-and-dogs but heaven hard. To translate literally from Hindi, it is raining rain. That's what Shudrak said in his famous play *Mrichhikatikam*: the rain is raining. There is nothing on earth or heaven which can fall like monsoon rain. So it has washed everything else right out of my mind.

It is August. I am reminded of the last chapter of *Chittacobra*. I felt I had to share this with you. Will you come to me tonight the way Richard came to Manu in the book. Will You? How can you tell, it is after all, in my mind.

I am sitting in the balcony listening to the drum and roll of rain in the otherwise silent dark night. Everyone has retired to bed. The three days in Thiruvanantpuram (Kerala) were gorgeous. How easily one gets used to the ocean and to serenity and happiness! When I got up this morning, I missed not seeing and hearing it. People like me who have lived mostly in the plains of Delhi are equally thrilled by the mountains and the sea. But the ocean in Kerala! That perfect round of the horizon seen from the balcony of my room upon first opening my eyes, it was for me truly therapeutic.

Remember you and I sitting in the Sea Lounge of the Taj Hotel in Bombay for hours? Everything seemed so simple and indestructible, though we knew it was neither. Or perhaps it was, the way it has remained fresh in our memories.

After a long time, I felt like writing a poem and did on a scrap of paper. I'll send it to you for what it is worth. The rain has now settled to a rhythmic beat. Content...just to be. Like me. Goodnight my love, hoping you shall come to me. No bidai, bondhu; stay with me.

M

K@crossroads.com to M
Aug 18, 2008

Maya, Maya,

Your email came through just as I was reading your earlier one, and thinking of you!

It is again August and it has been raining incessantly for three days!

Yes, my dear love, I will come to you this night as Richard did to Manu, with all the force my mind and heart can achieve. But it is not the name of Manu I will say when my head is again on your lap, but your beloved name—Maya—and you will hear me in your mind saying it over and over again, as we rediscover our love, so alive and so sharply remembered after all the years. I will come to you when I go to bed, and I will come to you again each time you wake me during the night— and you will! Waking or sleeping, I will be in your arms.

Better stop there, before I get completely carried away! I have just reread the last chapters of *Chittacobra,* and find my whole being responding to the beauty with which you describe us— probably more beautiful than the reality, but that is your precious gift as a writer.

Love,

K

`M@chaurasta.com to K`
20 August 2008

Dearest Kevin

Thanks for your lovely letter. We have to be content with what we have. So many times, one does not know one is happy till afterwards. So to ask for anything more than this benediction, which has allowed us to express our innermost thoughts to each other, would perhaps be greed.

You did not come to me—how could you, except in my thoughts?—but I did get your book yesterday evening. Thanks. The rain was still raining its august tumult when it arrived.

I have not read all of it yet, but I did read the chapter on your childhood and the sojourn in India. And of course I looked at your so correct photograph many times. You look different from what I remember of old, but a little like you were when we last met in London.

The childhood recall was a scream (pun intended)!

I have been to quite a few places you mention, and Vienna and Graz in Austria were some of the most cherished. I read about your Jewish composer uncle and was reminded of my very own secret treasure, a dear young man called Michael Weiss. I will tell you about him some day.

But for now Michael will have to wait. I need to recount back to you what you have called your most poignant memory, your Uncle Richard.

During our stay in Vienna, my parents became friendly with a gentle and distinguished man whom I called Uncle and who grew fond of me despite my faults! He was a musician and composer— not widely known but celebrated in his own community. He was to give me the most precious gift I have ever received.

It is a tune composed by Richard Nohrig to the lovely words of a lullaby by one Dettler von Liliecran. At the bottom of the sheets of music are the words: Composed by Mr.Nohrig—Harland—Austria February 1935 for Kevin Wilson (age 3 years).

It was in German but the last verse can be roughly translated as:

'Sleep my little one, the time is coming,
When the rain will fall, storm and snow will come.
Sleep while you may, in peace without care,
While you still can know rest and security.'

As he composed the music to those words, the storm that was to blow away the security of Europe and destroy the old world forever was growing more menacing. He perished in the gas chambers of Auschwitz. I was to pray for him there one day nearly half a century later.

This spoke so ardently to me that I want to store it in our shared memories, hence the quote. A little surprising that you did not mention him when you talked of Richard in *Chittacobra*. What an amazing coincidence that our Richard should have the same name as your beloved 'Uncle'!

I started reading the chapter on India with trepidation. One false note, a single undercurrent of condescension, would have damaged the image I have always cherished of you. Not my love, but certainly my esteem, of you, and of myself too. I am sure you understand. Thank you for writing the way you have about your time here. We are so transparent when we write without a target audience. I realize it is no more than a footnote in this book; still, sometimes a single sentence is enough to bare all.

Of course with your lucid and humorous yet emotive style, the book is an easy enjoyable read.

I am truly amazed at some of the other coincidences. The Omar Khayyam *Rubaiyat* you quoted was my favourite from early childhood, particularly in the original Persian that my father recited to us.

The rain has stopped and so must I.

Love,

M

K@crossroads.com to M
Aug 20, 2008

Maya, Maya,

Your letter made me very happy.

Ah, my Uncle Richard Nohrig, the gentle composer who perished in a concentration camp. I am glad you can now claim his memory as yours and it can become our shared memory. He and my parents played a great part in my commitment to tolerance.

As I say in my book, my conversion to the Christian faith and my early political education went hand in hand and inoculated me against the kind of Christian faith which turns people too heavenly minded to be earthly people.

But I am overjoyed that you found my chapter on India fair. The years in India are such a treasured memory, to which I owe so much—and then of course there was you! How could I be condescending? It was good to have your 'imprimatur'. But as you know, I learned my liberation theology while in India.

As for contentment, it depends on what you mean. I believe I am happy with who I am and what I do, but I am never content, if it means accepting things as they are. I accept with gratitude what you call the 'benediction' of our renewed contact, but it will not stop me asking for more, however remote that seems.

I love Omar Khayyam—I often bore my family by reciting reams of poetry, from Shakespeare through Wordsworth, to Rupert Brooke and G.K. Chesterton—yes, and a bit of Tagore too.

One more thing. In the mind of course, but I did come to you as Richard did to Manu last night.

'Lovers and madmen have such seething brains,
Such shaping fantasies,
That apprehend more than cool reason ever comprehends.
The lunatic, the lover and the poet are of imagination all compact.'

—Shakespeare's *A Midsummer Night's Dream*

THE OLD CRAZY INDEED!

With my love,

K

M@chaurasta.com to K
21 August 2008

Dearest,

That poem certainly seems to be about us!

I honour your parents for what they did in the town of Lodz to tear out your budding infant intolerance in one stroke.

To quote you: *The city of Lodz, though Polish, was home to a large nunmber of German origin whose loyalty to the Third Reich was increasing. My father spoke fluent German and I, too, was fluent as only a small child could be. I was sent to a local German kindergarten at the age of four.*

I was to be infected by prejudice there in a way that has, I believe, effectively inoculated me against it for the rest of my life.

After two months at school my parents were walking me home and took an unaccustomed route. As we were to enter a particular street I piped up, 'Don't go through this street. Many dirty Jews live here.' My kindergarten days ended abruptly. I was removed from school...and I was not allowed to forget.

So glad you were not! Otherwise you would never have come to India; we would have never met; I would not have become a writer and so on...there, the confession is out! I have acknowledged it in my new novel *Miljul Mann*, but not many people seem to get it! Tell the truth and no one believes it!

All my love,

M

K@crossroads.com to M
Aug 22, 2008

My dear honest love,

So I am not too immodest when I believe I played a part in your becoming what you are, as you did in making me what I am.

But yes, my parents had their share in it.

Love forever,

K

M@chaurasta.com to K
23 August 2008

No dearest you are not. I started on my very first novel, *Uske Hisse ki Dhoop* in 1974 (published exactly a year later in 1975) a day after I had met you (on Holi, not important; TMI as your daughters would say; but it helps me fix things in my mind). You asked me out of the blue 'what would your life have been if you were married to me?' Promptly, came my answer, 'I would have fallen in love with Naveen.' A good riposte but a lie—that would have never been.

But somehow, the exchange stayed with me and I started my novel with that as the theme. A woman divorces her husband to marry another, madly in love with her. Soon she finds his possessive love irksome and has an affair with her former husband and so on. She says to herself that all she wanted was a vacation and anyway love was no big deal. So different from *Chittacobra*. Surprising, isn't it, that no one found it objectionable in the way they did *Chittacobra*. I think passionate love evokes either fear or envy in most 'reasonable' people, hence the recoil.

Actually *Uske Hisse ki Dhoop* was published while we were still in touch, but of course it was in Hindi. But I do remember your reading a story of mine on the same theme in English, (in fact, the novel was developed from it) *A Few Hours*, while sitting next to me in Taj's Sea Lounge in Bombay and finding it quite shocking. Remember, I used to live in Bagalkot, Karnataka then, but came to Bombay often, where we met, mostly at the Taj?

K@crossroads.com to M
Aug 23, 2008

Dearest,

Of course I remember. The Taj Sea Lounge, the story, you, everything! But I was not shocked by the story. All I said was that it was unusual. Surely it was, and so must have been the novel. Has it not been translated into English?

K

`M@chaurasta.com to K`
23 August 2008

It was. I did it. Called it *A Touch of Sun*. But it was not a good translation, though it got published. I intended to redo it but never got round to it. It's on my computer but I don't think I am ever going to do anything about it. Its old hat by now! The Hindi one is going strong in its nth edition though. Women love to live vicariously through it.

But I realize I said nothing about the lines on p.74 in my last mail. You say in them that you have loved only one woman in your life, your wife Lynda. Such are, my love, the pitfalls of writing autobiographies! Novels can be so much more objective.

And you tell me it is only a half-truth. So be it. It does not matter to me either way.

By the way I was rather amused by what you had to say about Shiva. I don't know whether you met him at all after we stopped seeing each other, but I had a few chance encounters with him. He has certainly changed!

He was the Environment Secretary when I was associated with the Centre for Science and Environment. Since you have been associated with environment and the Earth Summit, I assume you know of the maverick Anil Aggarwal, who used to be the Centre's Chairman. I did not come in direct contact with Shiva but the Centre did. So, in 1988, when I was trying to find you, I rang him at his office and asked if he knew your whereabouts. He said he did not, but was fairly decent and quite like his old self, albeit pompous.

But when I ran into him a few years later, at some do of the Centre with his wife, I found him entirely changed. Anil introduced us and he pretended as if Durgapur never existed. Two years ago, I ran into him, now retired, at India

International Centre in Delhi, again with his wife. He seemed almost afraid to be seen talking to a woman.

What I saw and knew of him during the Rajiv Gandhi era does not agree at all with your view of a selfless, non-power-hungry public servant. Quite the contrary. But people change.

By the way Rupert Brooke is another favourite of mine. Care to quote him?

I attach my own very meagre effort, written on the shore at Kovalam beach.

With love,

Maya

The Rock Unveiled

The white wave rushed headlong
Inviting the rock to fall
In its impetuous embrace
The rock tried but could not move
It was after all a rock
Immobility was its destiny.
The wave threw itself upon it
Come take one step it keened
Recognize the vehemence of my desire
The rock wept bitter tears
The wave thought they were all hers
Repulsed it turned back.
Don't go willed the rock in despair
Drown me so I can turn into you
I can move only if I cease to be
The rock wanted to shout
But could not

It was after all a rock
Silence was its vocation.
The wave heard only the beating
Of its own heart wild with blatant desire
It could not conjure the silence
To hear the rock's soundless prayer
With supernatural effort the rock moved
But the wave had already coursed back.
The setting sun was the only witness
It shrugged off the drama and went its way
The black rock stood rooted at a new spot
A mute shrine to its mutant passion.

K@crossroads.com to M
Aug 23, 2008

Dear one,

Sorry about Shiva. Certainly I remember him as very helpful, both in Durgapur and Calcutta. I once met him later when he was in Washington at the World Bank, and again he was friendly and of great help. Too bad if he has become pompous and misogynist!

Your poem was evocative for me. I have always loved the breakers, especially in a storm. That is something we never did together, though we were by the sea. It is good to see you writing poetry again.

As for the p.74 item, I was perfectly aware when I wrote it that I was not telling the whole truth—I knew that it was possible to love more than once—but each love had its own special character and colour—the colour of my being? Do tell me one day about Michael Weiss—I read his lovely tribute on the inside cover of *Chittacobra*.

Here is a bit of Rupert Brooke which speaks to me.

With love,

K

The Beginning

Someday I shall rise and leave my friends
And seek you again through the world's far ends,
You whom I found so fair
(Touch of your hands and smell of your hair!),
My only god in the days that were.
My eager feet shall find you again,
Though the sullen years and the mark of pain
Have changed you wholly; for I shall know
(How could I forget having loved you so?)
In the sad half-light of evening,
The face that was all my sun rising.
So then at the ends of the earth I'll stand
And hold you fiercely by either hand,
And seeing your age and ashen hair
I'll curse the thing that once you were,
Because it is changed and pale and old
(Lips that were scarlet, hair that was gold!)
And I loved you before you were old and wise,
When the flame of youth was strong in your eyes,
—And my heart is sick with memories.

M@chaurasta.com to K
24 August 2008

Kevin love,

Oh dear! I did not mean to run down Shiva. I know he was
always friendly and helpful at least in Durgapur. That was why

I found his later behaviour inexplicable. Not a misogynist, just afraid of his wife. A lot of arrogant men who marry late, are. But wasn't Shiva always rather pompous? That is one trait likely to grow with age. I remember someone remarking, wonder if he is like that in bed too! Not you, was it? No, someone else.

You are not far wrong about my poems being because of you even when they are not about us. I don't usually write poems. The few I wrote in the beginning were surprisingly, unlike my major work, all in English. So who for, or because of, but you! Later of course, after 1976 when you decided to go away, the poems were about us, though there was no us then. The first one was the 'The Night the Cactus Flowered.' I translated it into Hindi and put it in my play.

The Night the Cactus Flowered

I waited for you that night
The night the cactus flowered
Longing for you to come
Knowing my longing must wait
For the cactus to flower
Bigger and bigger it grew
The longing to be
Intense overpowering flowering
Not in a single burst of primal desire
Not in sudden disregard of containment
But softly trembling it grew to be
The flower on the cactus
I watched in ecstasy
A moment of wonder
Of longing realized
Hope fulfilled

For an hour it bloomed
The flower on the cactus
Before the night was over
It had ceased to be
Only the cactus remained
Longing for you to come
The flower to bloom
Another night

But dearest, the poem that seems truly to be about us is Rupert Brooke's, not mine. One's passion expressed as a quotation! You can take full credit for this poem, as I wrote it after so long, when you were back. I have enough critical sense to know I am no poet. I do it by instinct and for myself, and now for you.

More importantly, I have since been reading the political part of your book. I am deeply impressed by the quality of patience and negotiation that went into your seeing it through.

Also those were the years that spoke to me. No wonder you did not try to contact me then. You simply had no time! Fighting for your country is a full-time passion. To do it through non-violent and long-drawn out negotiation is an exhausting vocation.

To quote from the web, *Kevin's wisdom will remain relevant for a long time.* I agree. What you said in an earlier Assembly Hall event made me realize not only the intensity but the poetry of your passion:

I had a strange sense that I was surrounded, not just by the many hundreds present in the Assembly Hall, but by a 'cloud of witnesses' from the past. On the one side I felt the guardian presence of those Scots who in the 1320 Declaration told the King at Arbroath that he ruled 'subject to the consent of the realm,' and who pledged their lives 'not for honour, glory or riches but for freedom alone.'...To my other side I felt the presence of ghosts from my own past, those who had helped me in my pilgrimage and brought me to this time and to the convictions which I hold dear.

My love, I believe some of those ghosts were Indian! Gandhi most assuredly if I know you. Bose? No, maybe not. Tagore, perhaps! Even though Gandhi and Tagore differed on many things, both spoke to the spirit and if one did not follow blindly, one could choose wisely between them.

One needs a different kind of patience to hone and fine-tune a novel. That's what I am doing these days and seize upon any excuse to bunk it. Yet it pursues me like a demon. And I am suddenly at it at any hour of the day.

Oh dear, to have two passions at one time!

Ok love. Need to go now.

M

K@crossroads.com to M
Aug 24, 2008

My love,

Thanks again—I love reading your thoughts. And you are right about Gandhi being among my ghosts. Tagore too.

You say you are not a poet. I am no expert, but they seem to me both lovely and full of meaning—but I admit I may be a bit biased! Please send me all your poems. Like so many of them, and like *Chittacobra*, 'Cactus' left me feeling a deep love for you.

And you are right! Shiva always was a bit pompous, and I could see the trait getting worse over the years.

K

M@chaurasta.com to K
25 August 2008

Dearest,

I am watching a cricket match; making pancakes and listening to my granddaughter recite a drama text, at the same time! She is taking a test in drama for eleven year olds from Trinity College in Oct. so we have to constantly hear her declaim during the weekends.

Love,

M

K@crossroads.com to M
Aug 25, 2008

Darling,

Your life now sounds good—cricket, pancakes, and a lovely granddaughter declaiming drama. This is something I envy you—not so much the cricket and pancakes (though I would love to taste yours), but the granddaughter.

Love,

Kevin

M@chaurasta.com to K
25 August 2008

My dearest love,

It's good to talk about my pain, to write about it. Also to be aware of my imperfections and try and put them in perspective of a larger picture. I don't always succeed; fail more often than not. As for vanity or arrogance, in a way I am glad not to be free of it for it helps deal with life's blows.

Enough of philosophy or blethering. Let's talk of something else. I had been meaning to mention this for a while but it always slipped my mind when I was on this machine. Apparently the London Book Fair in April 2009 is going to focus on India. Guess some writers from India will be going there. Now, my usual way of dealing with such things is to do nothing except wish intensely that I would be invited by the powers that be. It works sometimes. Did last year for New York. So between you, me and the doorpost, I might just happen to see you if the Federation of Indian Publishers and one Susanna Nicklin of the British Council so conspire.

Goose-bumpy thought, darling, isn't it? Not likely to come true but we can dream like Omar Khayyam can't we?

Love,

M

K@crossroads.com to M
Aug 26, 2008

Dearest Maya,

If you do manage to come to London, that would be great, so I will keep my fingers crossed.

But, my love, I am facing a massive internal struggle. Once I wrote to you long ago 'One cannot always be torn in two'. Not for an instant do I regret having found you again, but here is my dilemma. At the moment I am well, and have been for years, but I have to face the fact that I have arterial problems, and the possibility is that I could have to go into hospital for a while. Don't worry, nothing is imminent or even likely as far as I know, but I am afraid of the hurt and damage it would do to Lynda, if she or one of our daughters found our emails.

The only idea I have is to find a trigger that warns you—
or me—to stop sending messages until another is received.
So here goes—if I send you an email with just one word
RICHARD, do not reply until you hear again. Should I do
the same for you?

I am trying this week to finish my book, so maybe that is
making me conscious of my mortality!

I love you.

K

K@crossroads.com to M
Aug 28, 2008

Are you OK my love? Just can't help it—I miss your sharing
yourself with me. I hope I have not stupidly caused you any
more pain than I have already.

I have read and reread *Chittacobra*, and the poems you sent
me. They do make me grateful to have known such love, but
also sorry for the hurt I caused. Maybe love and pain just go
together. I am just starting to read *Kathgulab*.

Come back to me!

K

M@chaurasta.com to K
28 August 2008

My dear K,

Your last email was like a rude wake-up call. Your suddenly not
wanting to be torn into two is bewildering! Frankly I don't
pay much credence to that. One loves more than one person
in different ways and I for one don't care what people, even

very dear ones, think of me after I am dead and gone. I have no love for my corpse.

I think you should hurry up and get an Independent Parliament for Scotland. It may cure you of being periodically torn in two!

As for *Chittacobra*, it's after all just fiction! Come, don't be maudlin.

M

K@crossroads.com to M
Aug 28, 2008

Dear Maya,

Maudlin— yes a good word, I must indeed have been feeling a bit that way, One thing I promise, my love, is to be honest with you and to open my heart and mind to you as fully as I can.

Love,

U no hu—the old crazy (still)

M@chaurasta.com to K
29 August 2008

Dear K,

I accepted this renewed tenuous relationship to give ourselves a chance to have a kind of serene happiness. Remember though, you voiced a hope or dream that we might meet again someday. I never gave that much credence.

But gradually, I did allow myself to indulge in the kind of fancy that I cultivate while writing fiction. The London Book Fair was part of such a fantasy. But just as I had finally come to terms and started enjoying the renewed relationship, you voiced your internal struggle. It came as a big jolt.

There was hardly any chance of my going to London. But now I might exert myself to make that possible. I am quite a contrary person, as you would know by now. But If I manage to go it will be solely for the sake of getting my due as a writer.

Do read *Kathgulab* to know me as a writer who can write about people who have nothing to do with you or me. It will probably release you from the burden of being the sole driving force behind the painful process of writing, which is both substitute and value addition to life for me.

Sorry for the prosaic panegyric. After all this, l can still say I love you and know you love me. I don't mind Crazy.

M

`K@crossroads.com to M`
Aug 30, 2007

Dear Maya,

Chittacobra may just be a work of fiction for you, but for me it is something to treasure for its honesty and truth. You and I were not 'just' fiction, and neither am I ready to believe that Manu and Richard were 'just fiction.' Fiction maybe, but for me so very much more. The same applies to your poetry, the 'forgotten papers.'

Of course I know that you are an accomplished writer—but let me retain my happy illusion—if such it be—that at least some of your writing, not forgotten, owes something to me and to our love.

Let it be quite clear. I am not in turmoil or anguish. I am very happy that we are in touch again even if there are occasional irritations.

Can we at our age be having a lovers' tiff?

Love,

K

M@chaurasta.com to K
30 August 2008

Why not a lovers' tiff at our age? I find it quite refreshing.

M

K@crossroads.com to M
Aug 30, 2008

I think I might have fallen in love with you?

Love,

Kevin

M@chaurasta.com to K
30 August 2008

Why the question mark?

M

K@crossroads.com to M
Aug 30, 2008

Good question! But then, why the 'might' or the 'I think'? You know that I KNOW.

For some reason, I am just remembering the yellow dress!

M@chaurasta.com to K
31 August 2008

My dearest love,

Happy birthday. At least I hope I have the date right. It is on 31st August isn't it?

Here is the story I promised to send you as a b'day gift: 'Woman of Sixty' in English translation. And of course, my love, untarnished by age.

You are welcome to any teenage tiffs you may feel inclined to have with me in your ripening old age. Though the real fun is making up in each other's arms. I hold you close and give you all the love your heart can cope with.

Irrationally yours,

Maya

K@crossroads.com to M
Aug 31, 2008

Thank you my love

I feel you holding me close, and love seems to flow between us like an electric current. And thanks, my Maya, for the lovely gift. A story as vibrant and soulful as *Chittacobra*...almost.

The ending in particular brought *Chittacobra* back so soulfully to me, that I feel impelled to quote it back to you:

"'Sixty year olds are free of social stigma,' she had written twenty years ago. Utter nonsense! Talk nonsense and the world hastens to read you. Talk sense and readers turn scarce. He must be thinking she is past sixty but still obsessed with colouring her hair. She paused as she passed by him to go up from the other staircase but kept standing. To hear what he wanted to say. He was sure to; had grown loquacious with age. One word out of him and she'd immediately go down instead of up. But he said nothing. They stood in silence. The time lived twenty years ago began to pulsate inside her. Soon it gushed out like a blast of wind and refused to settle down. She tried to throttle it with words. There is nothing more potent than words to kill fancy and longing. Ask when was the Church built, who built it, which people stood first on the balcony? Lovers perhaps? Star-crossed or full of confidence? No chance! Blasts of wind are not that fragile. The gust spiraled up and threatened to turn into a tornado.

Meet; separate; meet; separate... again and again and so...

They now stood together on the fifth floor balcony. An avid yearning filled her heart that he should take her in his arms; so they could fit in the same circle; so each may hear the other breathe. She did not wait for long. She spread her own arms and encircled him. He came and nestled on her bosom.

Then they went down the same staircase, together.

'Sixty-year-olds are free from social stigma'—that's a line from *Chittacobra*, isn't it? It is stamped on my heart and mind. I know of the quaint but romantic convention of Graz, that lovers have to go by separate staircases to the five floors of the church, meeting and separating on each balcony, till they reach the ever-narrowing top. It had always appealed to my romantic nature. But the way you've woven this story around this backdrop filled me with 'avid yearning' to go there with you and have you engulf me in your arms.

And now that you are not the diffident forty-year-old who baulked at expressing her love, but a sensual seventy—ten years more than sixty!

So fervently did I crave it, that I felt myself in your arms.

All my love,

Kevin

M@chaurasta.com to K
1 September 2008

Dear Love,

It must be early morning now in Stratford-upon-Avon, as it is afternoon here. This time difference seems quite symbolic. We seem to be either ahead or trying to catch up. According to the time on the mail, it was late night when you answered me. But where, here or there? I am a bit confused. Guess it's the time here. Then that was the time I went to bed with a book. I could feel you in my arms as I drifted to sleep so if you too found yourself in my arms, for once your time and mine were the same.

Love

M

K@crossroads.com to M
Sep 1, 2008

Dearest,

Yes, my email was apparently sent at 17.47 GMT (which is at present 18.47 as we are on Summer Time, an hour ahead). So yes, you are right. If you felt that close to me and in my arms, I was feeling it at the same time. Wonderful.

Love,

Kevin

P.S. After long deliberation, I have decided you may remove both the question mark and the word 'might'!

M@chaurasta.com to K
2 September 2008

Dearest,

How did you celebrate your birthday?

By the way, though 'Woman of Sixty' is not about you, it starts with the quotation from *Chittacobra* that a woman of sixty can do whatever she wants...so, with a little imagination and a lot of ego, neither of which you lack, you can easily believe it to be about you.

Love,

M

K@crossroads.com to M
Sep 2, 2008

Dearest,

My birthday celebrations were modest and family.

I am not vain enough to believe that everything you wrote had me somewhere—but a man can dream! I was a bit miffed when you called *Chittacobra* 'just fiction'. My problem was not with the word 'fiction' but with 'just'. For me, it is much more.

Sleep well, my love,

K

M@chaurasta.com to K

2 September 2008

You have said many things about *Chittacobra*, all very poignant. But today I want to say to you the lines which you have never commented on, but which are the essence of *Chittacobra,* articulating the agony of two people to whom Time means different things.

As Manu says, '*It was easy for someone constantly on the move to wait. What about the one who was fixed at one place? How could one make him understand what it was to have the sun rise in front of the same window every morning...he whose window opened in a different country each morning and evening?*'

For me these are the most crucial lines.

That's why I envied your globetrotting, not because you saw different places but because you had defeated Time inasmuch as it conferred a similitude or routine for a person fixed at one place...

I have not quoted the entire para. You can read it. It'll help you understand why it is fiction which encompasses all humanity and not just us. Ok I am willing to take out the 'just'. It's good for my ego.

K@crossroads .com to M

Sep 3, 2008

Maya Maya,

Allow me to disagree with you. I can't argue about your fictional characters, but as far as you and I are concerned, I might have been on the move and you fixed at a place but I waited for you with equal if not greater intensity. It was always I who came back to you, did I not? Being on the move certainly made it easier for me to move back to you again and again. But the wait was never easy. Worthwhile certainly. And now, Maya we are both on the move, so do you no longer wait?

But as long as *Chittacobra* is not just fiction, I can put up with your fictional characters.

To quote from 'Woman of Sixty', we might have gone up the church by separate staircases, we returned together and as you predicted, after we had turned sixty.

So with Love and Waiting,

K

M@chaurasta.com to K
3 September 2008

Dearest,

Ok then, let's agree to agree that we are both each other's fool and have been for years.

You ask about my birthday. Well, there are no plans at all. Haven't had a birthday to speak of for so long. Somehow Ashwin and family are never with me then. My fault since I prefer to come to Bangalore in July–August. My daughter-in-law sends me a young looking outfit and my kid sister and her daughter take me out to dinner. Even my 60th b'day, which you might know is a big thing in India, got celebrated by default.

1998, my sixtieth birth year was an eventful one. My first grandchild, a lovely daughter was born early January 1998. My writer elder sister passed on, end of July. I spent August–September in Bangalore and returned to Delhi in October with only one wish for my b'day: somehow to escape the duty wishes of the extended family and friends. My wish was granted. I was invited to Jodhpur to address a literary gathering.

As it was my first public appearance after the death of my famous sister, I spent the rest of the day after my lecture answering questions about her from every literate/literary female in town (not too many fortunately).

The Rajmata (Queen mother) of Jodhpur gave a dinner for a few of us at Umaid Bhawan, one of the most beautiful palaces ever built. When she realized from the flap of my book that I was turning sixty that day, she graciously had a thumri (my favourite classical form) sung for me in the Baradari, (an open courtyard with twelve pillars). The architectural harmony apparently results in perfect acoustics and resonance, calming the nerves. Somewhat like the pyramids I guess. It did cure my raging headache, brought on by hordes of women condoling with me.

My only regret was that I was in a crumpled sari and looked like a frump. To escape them, I had gone for a long walk in the evening and, as usual, got lost, so had had no time to change or brush my hair, when the car arrived to take us to the palace. The Rajmata very kindly said that was exactly how she expected a 'great' (ahem) writer to look! Believe me, it was no consolation!

Anyway the Baradari with its calming influence helped me write a love story on my return, 'Woman of Sixty', naturally.

As always there are no plans for my b'day. That had been my younger son's department. He always managed to make me feel twenty, and extraordinary in every way.

In any case, once you are sixty, the next milestone is seventy-five, not seventy. So who knows, if I live to be seventy-five, chance might have a scion of another defunct royal family give me dinner in some fabled baradari.

Ah yes, I did get a lovely gift. Ashwin happened to be in Australia and got me a lovely opal. That was special! I have been wearing it since in a ring. He had also shifted to a new house he had designed himself, an environment-friendly place, whatever that may mean. He has solar heating and rain harvesting and trees that are never pruned. The last I have never been happy about.

Hope you have not begun to get bored with my unending non-fiction stories.

Love,

M

`K@crossroads.com to M`
Sep 5, 2008

Bored, my love? Never. I laughed out aloud at your description of your sixtieth birthday and especially at the Rajmata's view of your crumpled sari and frumpishness (though I don't believe the latter), as being what she would expect of a great writer. All bohemian then, are you now? Anyway, if we both make it that long I will try to devise some way of accidentally ensuring your seventy-fifth is as memorable!

Not much to report here. I am struggling with the final three chapters, the third part of my book 'Healing the Nations; Healing the Earth.' Incidentally, I heartily approve of the ecologically-friendly house. My laziness in gardening means I have a natural sympathy for those who do not prune trees!

Love,

Kevin

`M@chaurasta.com to K`
5 September 2008

Ah my love, the best part of writing fiction is that one is not expected to offer solutions. The readers are supposed to get inspired to find them, and if they don't, it's their funeral. We write not only of what is and what could have been, but also of what ought to be, but others have to devise the means to the end!

In India these days, people seem to prefer to read narratives with a litany of facts and ready-made solutions rather than literature. Pulp fiction is another matter because it absolves both writer and reader from the onerous task of thinking.

By the way, you didn't tell me whether you have ever been to Jodhpur or any part of Rajasthan. And did you ever meet Anil Aggarwal? I need to know what you thought of him.

Ok, won't take any more of your time away from your book!

Love,

M

`K@crossroads.com to M`
Sep 6, 2008

Dear M,

Since I am attempting a historical and theological analysis of the dilemma facing humanity, I cannot escape the obligation to offer solutions, or at least suggest the basis for a way forward. For example, a new education system designed to use modern information technologies, but also enable people to use the torrent of information responsibly and think for themselves. Also the need for stronger reformed global political institutions, capable of controlling globalization for human goals, etc. etc.

Yes, long ago—even before we met—I did make a brief visit to Jodhpur and Udaipur, and even have an ancient faded 8 mm film to prove it. I remember how impressive they were, but frankly little of detail. My memories are vague—in contrast to those of every time with you.

As for Anil Aggarwal, I do not think we ever met. Would it be likely that I had?

Go on being both creative and happy—I hope the two are compatible!

Love,

Richard (I feel a little fictional in response to your email)

M@chaurasta.com to K
7 September 2008

Dearest,

I'm so glad you are saying these things in your book. A new education system is what I have been harping on in every column, article, talk and even stories and novels of mine (particularly *Kathgulab* and *Anitya*) till everyone is quite sick of it. And I began much before Amartya Sen.

Following my belief in equitable education I have opposed caste and gender reservations, which makes me very unpopular. I hope your treatise manages to make some fatheads rethink.

Anil Aggarwal was the prime mover behind the use of CNG vehicles in Delhi, and for putting the Third World's view on climate change before the world. He was at the Rio Conference so I thought you might have met him.

With all his qualities as a rebel thinker, innovator and caring friend, he was a difficult man to get along with and foul-mouthed. He was diagnosed with brain cancer in 1994 and did his hammering of the establishment, forcing it to take action as a man in a hurry. He died a few years later.

The kind of global support we received during his illness and treatment in France, USA and later at an Ayurvedic centre in India made me think anyone concerned with ecology would know him. I was just interested in knowing what someone like you would have thought of him.

All the best for your book.

Love,

M

K@crossroads.com to M
Sep 8, 2008

My dotter keeps telling me that the way to reach people is not by theories and theology, but by stories—so, my dear love, you most certainly are doing more to help change this sad world than I am! The more you write to me of your feelings and thoughts, the more I feel in harmony with you. I can never regret our lovemaking being so complete, but I do regret that it did not give us enough time to know each other more in other ways.

I am glad that you agree with me. But how could you not, being so perceptive and brilliant!!

I realized that I knew the name Anil Aggarwal—probably from the time I was setting up the Scottish Environmental Forum to prepare for the Rio Conference. I passed up the chance to go, to get our Regional Council to sponsor a group of young people—so probably missed the chance to meet him.

Enjoy Bangalore. For now, just love,

K

M@chaurasta.com to K
9 September 2008

Dearest,

I am stuck at a crucial point regarding the end of my novel.
Always a tricky matter. One I always keep feeling afterwards I
have made a hash of. Been awake the whole night thrashing it
out in my mind till I am absolutely done in.

So will write after a while. It will come to me soon hopefully.

Love,

M

K@crossroads.com to M
Sep 11, 2008

Dear one,

Wish I could help—but I am with you as much as I can be,
holding you and giving you peace, and trying to make you
sleep in your exhaustion.

Let me know how the dilemma is resolved.

Love,

K

M@chaurasta.com to K
12 September 2008

My love,

There is light at the end of the tunnel.

By a strange coincidence or divine intervention—though I
don't think the Almighty has time for such small matters—a
writer/editor friend of mine from Mumbai came to Bangalore

and stayed a block away. I gave her the MS to read and she got through it in two days. We then had a talkathon for hours. After two more sleepless nights and by taking her incisive advice, largely by doing the opposite of what she suggested, I have finally arrived at a resolution. You can't imagine how exceptional it is to get a non-partisan and sensitive opinion on a novel.

I have decided to put in the last chapter as an epilogue with an interesting title, which leaves a lot to the imagination. I call it 'Mann se utre zameen par aaye'. I wish I knew how to make it sound as musical in English. Roughly it'll be 'From Fantasy Brought Down to Earth'. See what I mean!

I think I have solved the problem of leaving the story of my sister's life and, by default, mine, in the middle in a kind of no-man's-land. To continue would have made it tedious. I also ran the risk of resorting to half-truths or telling things my sister would not have wished told.

My friend agrees! I wrote the redrafted last chapter last night. When I finally went to sleep, I felt you very close to me. Maybe you were the one who helped.

What is the name of the shop in London where you bought *Chittacobra* and my other book? Nobody has any idea, so you are the expert!

Bye for now.

Love,

M

`K@crossroads.com to M`
`Sep 12, 2008`

Maya Maya,

Hallelujah—I am very happy that you are finding your way through the jungle. Incidentally, though I do not claim a personal and intimate acquaintance with the Almighty, I feel sure that He (or She) is perfectly able to be interested in what you do and create.

The London bookshop is called Bookshelf.

I am away for the weekend, returning Monday evening, to speak at a meeting organized by the Campaign for an English Parliament. We Scots are good at telling the English what to do. After all, we ran the Empire for them. (Sorry dear!)

Sleep well again—and somehow I will be there.

Love,

Kevin

`M@chaurasta.com to K`
`13 September 2008`

Thanks love. If Bookshelf has *Chittacobra* and *Country of Goodbyes,* published by the worst distributors possible, it will have any book from India!

How's your book progressing? Let me know when you are back from picking up the pieces of the empire!

With love to my dear crazy one,

M

K@crossroads.com to M
Sep 13, 2008

Hi Love,

Just off to Bournemouth to continue my task of reforming the world. Is that fantasy or reality?

Come to think of it, which are we? Manu and Richard or Maya and Kevin? I like the idea that in the end we move from fantasy to get down to earth. But both are real.

As for the empire, you do realize that my title of CBE stands for 'Commander of the Order of the British Empire'. I have never as yet been called upon to command anything, but I would expect you to address me deferentially as Commander!!

But you have awarded me a title that I much prefer—DCO (stands for Dear Crazy One).

Love,

Kevin CBE, DCO

M@chaurasta.com to K
16 September 2008

Guess you are home, my love.

I don't know what's happening in India. Now the bomb blasts in Delhi. It is inexplicable to me. Why is India a target? What have we done? We have never occupied or attacked any country, Islamic or otherwise. Of course, there have been riots within the country and they are equally illogical to me. Who gains from it and what is it they want from us? Who in the name of God is responsible for the madness? All this is supposed to be the result of that one act, the demolition of the Babri Masjid!

Then the attack on the churches in Mangalore in Karnataka! Has everyone gone mad!

Just before someone asked me to turn on the TV and see what was happening in Delhi, I had been truly peaceful.

So...I went and stood under the tree called akaash mallige (sky jasmine); so called because it's a tall tree with fragrant jasmine-like white flowers blooming at the very top. When there is a stiff breeze along with rain in August–September, as there is almost every day, the flowers fall like blessings from above. On one's face, if one stands under it and looks up at the sky. As I did. We had planted this tree in front of our house in Bangalore in 1998 when Ashwin built it, in memory of the lost children. The flowers caressed my face and I came back to write to you.

But again I do not know what to say.

So...just love.

M

K@crossroads.com to M
Sep 16, 2008

Dearest Maya,

Like you, I heard of the bomb in Delhi with total bewilderment, though I knew you were in Bangalore and not in danger. Why India? Well, there is no logic here. I can understand, even if I cannot condone, those who use force as a means to some political end—but those who kill and maim in the name of God seem utterly despicable and unforgiveable. I use the world deliberately, for Jesus speaks of the 'unforgiveable sin' as being when evil is seen as righteous.

I suppose the only cause I can think of would be Kashmir, since so many Muslims link it with Palestine as two examples of a global conspiracy against Islam. The very name of Pakistan includes Kashmir—and you know my feelings about Pakistan—the State which should never have existed.

Your feelings under the tree reminded me of Gandhi's words *'I can see that in the midst of death, life persists, in the midst of untruth, truth persists, in the midst of darkness light persists. Hence I gather that God is life, truth, light. He is love.'*

Love,

Kevin

M@chaurasta.com to K
21 September 2008

My dear love,

You are the only person who can tell me this.

Was there a time when I was a carefree, even careless person, looking forward to the future unafraid, wanting to try new things, unmindful of consequences; above all with a capacity to be happy without being afraid of being happy?

Dear love, how I long to be that person again. I must have been a happy, carefree person, otherwise you could not have loved me. I feel the same zest and tingle of excitement when I hear from you and I want to believe I am that person I remember vaguely.

My dearest, keep writing now and then, even if you don't hear from me immediately. Hearing from you has become my lifeline.

In love,

Maya

K@crossroads.com to M
Sep 21, 2008

Dearest, I think you must know the answer to your first question. Yes, when we were together, the woman I loved was all the things you say.

I suppose I always knew there were depths in you that I had hardly begun to know, but you were certainly alive and happy—and not afraid to be. If you don't remember the person you were, I am happy to remind you, in detail!

I can understand the events in your life have taken away that happiness—but in the end it is internal not external, and I remain sure that the real Maya is there waiting to be reborn

My God, I sound like an agony aunt in a magazine, doling out cheap advice!

Can I really be your lifeline across so many miles and years? Does that not have to come from those who have consistently loved you and been with you all those years?

You have my love.

Kevin

K@crossroads.com to M
Sep 24, 2008

Just to say I am thinking of you, and hope you are indeed happy.

Love,

Kevin

M@chaurasta.com to K
29 September 2008

My dear K

Just wanted to say that my 21st Sept. mail was never actually meant to be sent.

I go a little crazy as my son's death anniversary approaches and I write things only to erase them. They help me get over the hump. I don't know why I chose you as the straw to clutch... perhaps because Michael Weiss, who shared my feelings, and had consistently written on that day, wasn't going to this year.

It was blurred vision I guess which made me press 'send' instead of 'discard' and you got the mail. Consider it unsent.

What could you have possibly said but what you did.

Will write when I am more in command of myself.

K@**crossroads**.com to M
Sep 29, 2008

Dear Maya,

It is so good to hear from you again. I am glad you pressed the wrong button for I want to know and understand your feelings, be they sorrow or joy. So I refuse to consider it unsent. Please never feel that there is anything you need to hide from me. I do so want you to be the happy, wonderful, carefree person you were in my arms, and I know that underneath it all, you still are!

Love,

Kevin

M@**chaurasta**.com to K
10 October 2008

Dear K,

I am back from a conference at Mumbai.

I spent the last evening and night with a childhood friend close to the Taj Hotel. I was suddenly assailed by the memory that you dropped me back at their place late at night once after dinner at the Taj and we kissed. I am a little wary of memories now, but can't help asking, do you remember?

Love,

M

K@crossroads.com to M
Oct 10, 2008

Yes indeed. Memories are a bit to be wary of—I have precious memories of many times we were together—though I confess I do not remember kissing you goodnight at the flat. What I do have very vivid memories of, are our being together in the Taj hotel—you can fill in the rest.

I know you have many things to do and think about—but just send me a line or two when you have time.

Love,

K

M@chaurasta.com to K
13 October 2008

Dearest K,

Did we really spend a whole night together at the Taj? One night at a beach hotel in Bombay, yes, but otherwise it was mostly 'Love in the afternoon!'

The midnight kiss in my friend's apartment had an added thrill because her husband, also a childhood friend whom I admired, but with whom I had a running argument for nearly thirty years, was sleeping in the next room, unaware of the goings-on under his roof.

We finally made a pact not to argue after he had a heart attack in 1990 and a mutual friend insisted I must have caused it. It fell to me to cuddle him in my lap while his wife drove us to the hospital. Not knowing what else to do, I kept intoning the Gayatri Mantra. He insisted later that it had saved his life, though I'm sure it was my atrocious accent which made him refuse to kick the bucket till he had pointed it out to me.

That he would have been surprised if not shocked, added spice to the goodnight kiss.

Goodnight.

M

K@crossroads.com to M
Oct 16, 2008

Maya, Maya (sung!)

Did I ever sing 'Edelweiss' to you? Must have, because I can never hear the tune without thinking of you.

I want to hold you close—I know that's what you want too—but it is a bit hard over 10,000 miles.

Love,

Kevin

M@chaurasta.com to K
19 October 2008

Dearest,

The way you remember things and the absorption you must have had in me comes as partly a pleasant surprise. Deep down of course I must have known it.

I can understand that the sudden intensity of my feeling would have frightened you into cold rationality. I am talking of my 21st Sept mail.

You are after all a politician and British to boot! Touché! The trouble with rationality is that it hardly ever serves the purpose because the reaction it produces is anything but rational. I am getting terribly tied up, see what rationality does.

This is the pre-Diwali festive season which includes gambling with the family. I was up until 2 a.m. the last two nights, playing flash, straight gambling, so am a bit groggy. Did not make any money, but did not lose either, as I used to at one time. So I guess I'm no longer lucky in love!

I have been invited to read my paper on 'Writing the Self' at a conference on Writing the Future in South Asia, whatever that may mean. That's the best part of literary conferences; you can make them mean anything. Like Humpty Dumpty in *Through the Looking Glass.*

Good night for now.

M

K@crossroads.com to M
Oct 27, 2008

HAPPY BIRTHDAY MY LOVE—THINKING OF YOU

M@chaurasta.com to K
27 October 2008

Thank you. I thought you had decided to call it quits when I did not hear from you on my actual birthday two days ago. So your wishes are more than welcome now.

Love,

M

`K@crossroads.com to M`
`Oct 31, 2008`

Is all well? I have been looking forward to a reaction to my terrible picture!

Love,

U No Hu

`M@chaurasta.com to K`
`31 October 2008`

My dear Kevin,

All's well. It was Diwali! Family time! I was busy with nieces and nephews and their families.

Your picture, of course, was a lot different from your picture in my memories. Though not very different from the last time we met. It was most certainly not terrible. Just stamped by time as it should be. And quite awe-inspiring in the ceremonial robes of Midnight Mass.

But I need to say something else. In continuation of my letter of 21st Sept and your reaction to it. It has been on my mind and I want to clear the air.

You remember the last lines Rhett Butler says in that mother of pop novels, *Gone with the Wind*? 'Frankly my dear, I don't give a damn.' The last couple of months, I have been chanting that as a mantra instead of Om Namah Shivaya. No offense, but frankly my dear, I don't give a damn about your doubts or sense of right and wrong. I don't see how our corresponding can cause any hurt or damage to people we love. If a human heart cannot accommodate that much love, it is neither very human nor much of a heart.

I'll say to you what I said to Michael Weiss, a boy my son's age, a stranger, who just happened to come by during the most catastrophic time of my life. A few days after my son died

He did not have much English being an Austrian, also Jewish, as I told you earlier. A fine painter, an innovative musician and training to be a doctor (aren't they all in Vienna)! He was here to work at a leprosy hospital in Chennai during the summer vacation. I met him again before he left for Pokhra in Nepal where he read *Chittacobra* in German, hence the tribute, as you called it, on the flap of a later edition. It was much more than a tribute. He was speaking from his soul to mine as no one ever had.

Not even you, though you wrote to me with genuine heartfelt feeling when you learnt of my tragedy, from the Indian High Commission in London. That was soon after we had met in London, you remember of course. Among other things, you asked me not to withdraw from you. I don't think I answered, but I was touched and felt you close to me. But there were too many fears strangling me and I could not answer. I did not withdraw deliberately, it just happened. And then coincidently, your later letters went astray. A conspiracy of fate or a coincidence, who could say...like Michael Weiss?

Now, when I look back I wonder how could a total stranger understand so intimately what was in my heart and mind. For long I did not even think of that; it was so natural.

Write, I told him, when you want to. All his letters afterwards began with the words, 'Now I want...'

For nearly eight years, every time I thought why would a young man write to someone as old as I, his letter came; as if my thoughts had reached him. Michael was twenty-six, the exact age my son was when he died and Michael came to me.

He later gave up medicine and became a painter. In fact he had sent me a sketch of a cured leprosy patient from Chennai after his first two visits to me but I did not think that it would become his vocation or one of his vocations. He also played an ancient musical instrument called Saaz. Later he went to Japan and took a vow of silence to learn classical theatre including Noh. And other things like that...there were many unfathomed depths to him.

Then a few years later, his very young sister Anna committed suicide. The last I heard from him was to say he was going on a pilgrimage for her. No more. I don't know where he is or if he is. I am afraid to find out. For all I know, with all his talent he might be a very famous man and easily traceable on the web.

But...if he wanted to, would he not have written... after all he wrote to tell me of his sister Anna and also to say that my letter of shared grief had helped him. He was still with me but then the pilgrimage...and I never came to know why that vibrant young spirit had killed herself. Also I am not that good with Google so even if I try I might not succeed in tracing him. As you did me, God bless you...

But the truth is that I have never tried.

Who knows, one day I might open the door of my house and find him there! I'd take him in my arms and hug him to free him of all cares. But why should he have cares...he would be a famous painter or musician or actor or all three together...or else a mendicant? Who knows! Whichever way it might be, no vow lies between us to prevent me from holding him close like my lost son and soul mate...the true Sufi mashooq.

Before Michael went on to do other things, he did a fair sized painting for me in memory of my son, whom he had never met but perhaps knew better than anyone except me. It was a Japanese print and he sent it to me from Vienna by ordinary post. Surprisingly it reached me and hangs in my living room.

It shows small children being taken out of their coffins and buried again. I don't know the religious implication. I have never tried to find out and I don't want to know.

For a long while all I saw in it was a red flower. Then gradually I saw a coffin and the print of the face of a man. There was grief and also hope and hopelessness: resurrection or rebirth, whatever one wanted to see. I saw all of them but above all saw my son, recreated by Michael, yet lost forever. So I wept and wept and did not stop weeping for a whole day.

I feel a great need to tell you more about Michael, his sudden appearance in my house, his sensitivity and also his antecedents. I had met his uncle, William Goldman, a Professor of History during a seminar in 1988, the first time I had gone abroad for a literary event, in Dubrovnik, former Yugoslavia. We connected well as co-passengers do on a ship; but we did not correspond or keep in touch.

Five years later in July 1993, when I decided to take a trip alone to Austria on my way back from a conference in Germany, I wrote to him and asked him if he could meet me in Graz. He did for a day and showed me the sights, not from a touristy point of view, but as only an astute historian could, with an incisive and humorous perspective. I never realized he was Jewish, but why should I have. It was, after all, 1993. But perhaps I should have, because I was coming from Germany where they had taken me on an obligatory tour of the concentration camps. But Prof Goldman did tell me of Vienna's deal with Hitler, whereby Hitler agreed to spare its demolition if he could have Graz instead. He showed me the ramparts of the ruined forts of Graz, but more significantly, took me to the church with two staircases which met on every floor and separated again.

Little did I know that just two months later, my world would come crashing down. That I would turn from a gregarious cheery woman to a stone. Goldman had no idea of what or how I was doing but when his nephew Michael Weiss decided to take a trip to India, he told him to be sure to meet me in Delhi. He gave him my address and I guess not my phone number; I don't think the mobile phone had yet been invented; at least it had not come to India.

Anyway... Michael did not call. He just dropped in one evening! Little knowing that he was walking into a house of mourning, or about to come face to face with a woman, more dead than alive, who hadn't slept for a week and walked around like a robot.

He came in, young and vital, to hear from my niece about what had happened. He saw me sitting rigid and mute on the sofa before my son and his wife's picture. He walked over, came and sat beside me. Then he took me in his arms without saying a word. And would you believe it I put my head on his shoulders and went to sleep. He spoke to the soul within the stone I had become and filled it such empathy and succour that I came back to life and, like a newborn, went to sleep. He came again the next day with everyday ordinary flowers that he had picked from a wayside garden and gave them to my son and his wife. There is no other word for it. He did not put them ritualistically on the table on which their picture stood; he did not hand them over to me; he gave it to them as if to living people.

He told me he was going to Pokhra in Nepal for a few days. Mountains, lakes and solitude! That's where I want to go...I whispered. He said you will. He then asked for the German *Chittacobra*, (his uncle must have mentioned it) and said he'll write to me as he read it. He did and I felt I was in Pokhra with him.

He came once more before he left for Austria. He seemed destined to come on catastrophic days. My elder sister had had a heart attack and I had spent the day in the hospital with her. I came home to a pile of dirty dishes and no help. I had time only to prepare kadi chawal. You know what kadi chawal is, of course having lived in India for so long. And of course, like any Indian woman of my generation, I had to ask him if he wanted to eat anything! When he said yes, it threw me in a tizzy. Then I remembered that someone had brought chocolate barfi to my sister in the hospital. That's what we Indians excel at, bringing unsuitable food to the sick. My sister had not only had a heart attack, she was a heavy diabetic—so what better gift than a box of sweets! I offered them to Michael; after all he was from chocolate-crazy Vienna. He politely refused, said his grandfather had fed him so many chocolates in his childhood that he had an aversion to them. He could not eat anything with a hint of chocolate and this was solid chocolate plus thickened milk! I was still wracking my brains about what to give him when he quietly picked up a bowl and filled it with kadi. He sat in my kitchen, eating it with relish and said it was delicious. This time it was I who took him in my arms and hugged him tight till he said he was leaving for Vienna the next morning. The earth stopped spinning and my grip loosened. I had to sit.

He sat at my feet and said, 'I need to ask you something. If I leave medicine, it'll be a great blow not only to my parents but all my uncles, the whole family. And yet...I want to play music, paint, write...don't know exactly which...but what do you think...should I continue with medicine or...?'

My brain cried out, 'Do medicine. You will make a wonderful doctor. Who else would opt to work in a leprosy hospital, draw sketches of the patients and write with such poetic feeling about them?'

What I said was, 'You have the soul of an artist. Choose music or art. Your family would understand. After all they don't force you to eat chocolates, do they?'

He got up, embraced me and said, 'I'll write.'

That's when I said, 'Write when you want to.'

I have already told you the rest. He wrote when he wanted to...the important thing was that he wanted to. That he could write to me about his young sister's suicide as naturally as he offered flowers to my dead children or held me in his arms or painted an abstract painting, both poignant and mystical.

So I repeat to you, write when you want to. It is up to you to decide what to do. For myself I think my heart is big enough to give love to lots of people without bothering about right or wrong. That's why people write. To play havoc with the world's accepted sense of right and wrong.

In a lighter vein, I must confess I had a romantic, silly notion that you might make my birthday memorable in some way. Didn't you say that? In a way you did, by making me younger by two days! So, thanks.

Love (wrong or right I don't know)

M

K@crossroads.com to M
Nov 3, 2008

Dearest Maya,

I envy you the freedom of saying 'I don't give a damn'. Of course there can be no harm in our corresponding—but I cannot pretend that it does not bring out deep feelings for you that I have had all these years despite my long silence.

My problem has always been my upbringing in Scotland's Calvinist society, with all its inhibitions, plus the fact that I am a minister, sworn to uphold the values of my faith. Maybe if I had your creative gifts I could express this and heal it. I am just too damned logical!

My feelings for you, and my precious memories, are indelible. If you can accept that, you will just have to accept my occasional blethers.

Thanks for the evocative pen-portrait of Michael. You had often mentioned him, and I could see how important he had been in your life, so was glad and moved to have a picture of him as a person.

Love,

Kevin

M@chaurasta.com to K
4 November 2008

My dear Kevin,

Tell me one thing since you are a minister upholding the values of your faith: Does God punish one for breaking an impossible promise made under agonizing stress to the extent of slaughtering the innocent?

This question has plagued me for a decade and a half. Don't take too long to answer. I need to know.

Maya

K@crossroads.com to M
Nov 4, 2008

Dear Maya,

I have no easy or glib intellectual answer to your question— but before I attempt any response, I need to ask you to explain it more. Of course I understand the agonizing stress and pain, but what is the impossible promise, and how broken?

Tell me if you can, and I will try, however inadequately, to respond. Meanwhile, just my love,

Kevin

M@chaurasta.com to K
5 November 2008

I am terribly sorry, Kevin.

It was an unfair question. But believe me, it is not an intellectual query. A glib answer is not what I need nor can it be given.

Let's say a child is ill and the mother under extreme stress happens to say in one of her prayers, 'if you spare him, God, I won't do something or the other'. The child gets well. Eight or nine years pass; she has forgotten all about it. She inadvertently does what she had vowed not to. Would God take away the child? Would you call that divine justice?

It does not matter what the promise was. People think of giving up all kinds of things dear to them in moments of agonizing stress. The point is, does God avenge a broken vow? Even by punishing the innocent? That is my question.

You can at best give your opinion, I know. But that would be at least a more expert opinion.

M

K@crossroads.com to M
Nov 5, 2008

Dear Maya,

Your question is not unfair. It is one that troubles many people in one way or another. So let me do my best—even if it not very good.

I simply do not believe in a God with whom we can make bargains, still less in a God of vengeance. God is love, which means both that He forgives freely, and that He is with us in our suffering and pain. When people say (as followers of Islam as well as many Christians do) that all that happens is the will of God and must be borne patiently, I want to shout at the top of my voice, NO! NO. To say that God is the cause of all that happens—or even worse, that we all deserve what happens to us—is to cut the nerve of real compassion for others. God can, I believe—and indeed have much evidence of this—bring good out of evil, and use suffering positively, but He does not cause it. For Jesus, sickness and pain were not things to be borne as God's will, but enemies to be fought.

But this, of course, leads us to the heart of the dilemma—the old problem of pain. How can a God, who is both omnipotent and loving, allow the suffering and death and horror that fill the earth? There are no easy answers, but I can say one thing.

Our misuse of the free will given to us by God is the direct cause of war, violence and suffering. But it was in a sense, the condition of love. He had to take the risk of creating beings genuinely separate from Him.

But what troubles me more is the feeling that you are not raising theoretical questions about other people's dilemmas, but sharing your own. If this is true, then share with me—and I will offer you no more doctrines, but simply my love.

Your

K

M@chaurasta.com to K
5 November 2008

Dear K,

Of course I am not raising theoretical questions. This is my own private hell and has been for fifteen years. I try to believe—after all Jain faith admits of only a benign nature, no superhuman figurehead or Godhood—so I *should* believe that God cannot seek vengeance. But...rational thought and faith desert me and I find myself back in hell for no logical reason.

Thank you for telling me that God is love. It follows that love cannot possibly cause pain. That helps.

M

K@crossroads.com to M
Nov 5, 2008

I am sorry my love, but I still do not understand and nothing you have told me explains why you think God could want vengeance, or what you believe you have done to make such vengeance even conceivable. You seem to be carrying a great load, not just of pain, but of guilt, as if some act or failure of yours was somehow responsible for what happened.

If God is indeed love, as I believe with all my heart, He offers the freedom of forgiveness. I often say a prayer that we used in Coventry Cathedral,

Teach us good Lord, how to forgive and be forgiven,
that we may be at ease with one another and at ease with you,
and may walk unafraid in the way of obedience to you.

Love,

Kevin

`M@chaurasta.com to K`
6 November 2008

Oh my dear,

Put in cold words, it sounds so melodramatic.

I have done nothing terrible at all. Just broken a minor promise I made in my prayers when my son was seriously ill, saying I won't do this or that if he was spared. Then I forgot all about it and remembered it only after I had lost another son. When people talk of vows made before God, that minor transgression comes back to haunt me and plays havoc with my balance and equilibrium.

Relax, I have committed no crime. Wish I had though. Now that I have put it in words, it sounds so foolish that I am quite ashamed of my fancies.

Vengeance is far too melodramatic a word. It's just that I have been angry for so long that I sometimes indulge in verbal violence. There is pop psychiatry for you. Surely you can understand that. Michael did. But then he was studying to be a psychiatrist!

I am a Jain. We have an annual festival called Chima Diwas, a day on which we formally ask each other's forgiveness. Hope I have the humility to ask for forgiveness for my minor and major transgressions. If not I can always ask for forgiveness for that!

You know, my love, I have had such an awful lot of preaching done to me after the tragedy. All the while they spoke, oh so eloquently, I kept thinking, if only I could weep. The more they talked, the more my heart turned to stone.

The one doctrine which appealed to me was the karmic theory of Hindu philosophy, where you chose to act, and took the consequences of your actions; but fortunately in another birth. So there was no way to establish a connection between cause and effect. It appealed to my sense of the absurd and was consoling.

If you have read my novel, *Country of Goodbyes*, this is quite clearly spelled out. That's why the crazy Japs are translating it. The last part of the book, called Vipin, was written after the tragedy, the earlier parts just before.

Enough. Guess this would be a shrink's way of getting rid of a burden by talking about it.

Don't worry about me. When I do commit a crime—I seriously wish to kill quite a few people—you will be the first to know.

Love,

Maya

K@crossroads.com to M
Nov 8, 2008

My dear Maya,

Your last mail leaves me with a deep feeling of gratitude that you can share so much of yourself with me—but also frustration that there is so little I can say in response, except to assure you of my presence.

I admit I wondered whether the thoughts of Vipin about his freedom and the power of sorrow, in the last few lines of *The Country of Goodbyes* were not really and profoundly your own.

I have always worried that the fact that your great tragedy happened soon after our last meeting—that it might somehow spoil your feelings for me.

Love,

Kevin

`M@chaurasta.com to K`
15 November 2008

Oh my dear sweet love,

You have at last understood it. That was the promise I made in
'81 and broke in '93

Not to meet you again.

I had forgotten about it till I read Graham Greene's novel, *The
End of an Affair*, much later and it flashed through my mind
that I too had said some such words.

We had not met since 1976; there was no chance of our
meeting. I did not say that rationally or deliberately or even
aloud in my prayers. It was just something that went past my
mind.

I did not want to tell you, or maybe deep down, I did, to
explain why we could never meet even if I dared to live
the fantasy of going to London. I had refused an invitaion
earlier—I mean after 1993—to go there for the Vishwa Hindi
Sammelan.

M

`K@crossroads.com to M`
Nov 17, 2008

Dear dear Maya,

Yes, deep down, I have always feared that, but could not
possibly visualize the horror of it all for you.

But dearest, though the past can never be forgotten, it can be
forgiven—maybe we have reached the stage where we can be
at ease with it.

What we had together was not just love; it was a kind of
deep joy in each other. I would hate to think that in all the

problems and sadness of your life, all the demands that make you careworn, you have lost that joy—which is deeper than simple happiness.

Be good, and please, if you cannot be happy, be joyful.

Love,

Richard

M@chaurasta.com to K
1 December 2008

Talking of joy, why didn't you send me a birthday card or gift? I was so disappointed.

K@crossroads.com to M
Dec 1, 2008

Dear Maya,

Forgive me. I had marked your birthday in my diary, to be sure not to forget (for I am rather absent-minded I admit) but on the day when I went to send you a birthday greeting, my computer had somehow shut down, and I could not get into it.

I even thought of trying to ring you, but was not sure whether you would want that. With a little help from AOL I got back in the next day—so you presumably got it the day after that. I can only assume that my computer knew it was your birthday, and was playing a trick on me.

All I can say is that you were in my thoughts all day—I tried to send you a telepathic message—but obviously that did not work!

But I have a question. Why did this come into your mind now? I would be very sad if this had been troubling you ever since.

Meanwhile, India is very much in my prayers.

For now, just love,

K

M@chaurasta.com to K
2 December 2008

My dear child,

I am a writer. My mind is full of disjointed things and thoughts. It is what is called 'bhanmati ka pitaara' in Hindi (a loosely tied bundle of half-forgotten things or ideas or joys). One never knows which of them will get thrown to the top, when. I guess my mind sought refuge in this unfulfilled 'joyful' expectation in trying to get away from the horror all around.

Ringing me may not be a good idea. But I get so many cards from strangers that one more would not attract attention as long as you don't sign it Kevin. Richard's fine.

The important thing was the expectation, which was mine and mine alone, though you did promise to make it eventful. Never mind, a long time has passed and it was only your mention of 'joy' that brought it back to me.

My b'day passed quietly and unnoticed amidst Diwali celebrations. My son did send me a new monitor for the computer, so my poor old eyes are a bit more rested now.

Love,

M

K@crossroads.com to M
Dec 2, 2008

Namaskar Manu,

That's a response to the 'dear child' my love—though I admit I must look that way sometimes. I prefer 'lover' or any other epithet you care to use.

I know your feelings. In fact, we in Scotland have a name for it too. We say 'Ma heid's fu' o' broken bottles!'

Next week I am back up in Scotland again to speak at a meeting of an ancient Philosophical Institution in Paisley (where I was born and went to school) on the theme 'Devolution; Revolution; Evolution' I also have some other meetings, including a session with the First Minister, Alex Salmond.

Enough for now. As for joy—I can think of you and remember you only with joy.

Love,

Richard

M@chaurasta.com to K
3 December 2008

Dear Richard,

Have an evolved revolved trip to Scotland and your birthplace. Can one say devolved too, I wonder? One could always pay it extra to mean something.

Have fun with your roots and the government. Tell me all the new developments on your return.

I am busy answering the numerous letters of inquiry from the Japanese translator of *Kathgulab*. To date I have had about

200 of them. If you want to punish yourself through slow torture, ask a Japanese to translate your book!

Love,

M

K@crossroads.com to M
Dec 4, 2008

Dear M,

You seem to live at a level of highs and lows that I can only try to share. By comparison, my life seems rather bland and uninteresting, now that I am no longer the globe-trotter Richard was! I am off to Scotland tomorrow.

Love,

K

K@crossroads.com to M
Feb 7, 2009

Maya Maya Maya,

Sorry for the silence. My time in Scotland was extended, and on return my computer caught some virus which was finally corrected yesterday by two whiz kids from Chennai's Norton Symantec.

I am well enough, but troubled. On my way back from Scotland—by train—I did something I had not done before—I reread *Chittacobra* from start to finish, rather than dipping into it. Every page seemed alive with your laughter or wet with your tears—and mine. I know that I was the one to initiate contact after all these years, but I am scared of the Pandora's box, I seem to have opened; feelings I need to hide every day.

I am not the man you once loved. The hair through which you so loved running your hands is white and bit thinner. But I suppose for both of us that is nature at work.

Anyway, forgive this emotion, and tell me all the exciting things you have been doing and thinking.

With my love,

Richard (with *Chittacobra* on my mind)

M@chaurasta.com to K
15 February 2009

Dear troubled Kevin,

Last night I saw the movie, *Notting Hill,* in which this crazy guy Spike says, in reply to a friend bemoaning opening the Pandora's box, "I knew a girl called Pandora in school...but never got to see her...box...'

I think that an apt reply to what you have said. If reading *Chittacobra* makes you feel troubled, don't read it. It was, after all, written thirty years ago, three years after you chose to break our relationship. Though the feelings expressed in it are as real now as then.

The point is not *Chittacobra* but us, you and I, now. What relationship can we have? I thought we could be an emotional anchor to each other and fun to talk to and relate with.

I have far too many tragedies and problems in my life to cope with anything emotionally intense. And remember, the one time I reached out to you, in a moment of weakness, you drew back, telling me, and rightly so, that I had to rely on people who had loved me through the years!!

My problem is to locate those people! One is gone. The other son I dare not burden, as my husband does enough to push him to the edge.

But that's my problem, not yours.

As for us, though we cannot meet, we can still be friends, companions, romantic lovers, whatever you will, through email. Romance is a good invigorating thing at any age. I want ours to be a fun relationship, something to look forward to without baggage or strings, a mental link or support, whatever word you want to give it.

There have been so many stories told and films made about people falling in love through email, and then going on to meet, etc. Ours could be the unique case of meeting before and ending with love via email!

Forget *Chittacobra*. Remember me!

By the way, I use the antivirus from Norton Symantec for my computer. Well, that's sharing!

Love, M

K@crossroads.com to M
Feb 18, 2009

Dearest Maya,

On reflection I think 'troubled ' was the wrong word—except maybe in the way we speak of troubling the waters ('Like a bridge over troubled waters') It means, I suppose, moved, stirred up, flowing, no longer calm and still.

You are, of course, as usual, right. What about us here and now? I have to recognize that, compared to your life for the last sixteen years at least, mine has been smooth, with very little suffering and much fulfillment and happiness. I wish I could give some of it to you, or at least hold you—but I cannot— so yes, let it be a fun relationship, without too much baggage, though I hope you will always feel you can share with me even when it is not fun—and I can do little to help. So let us be indeed romantic lovers—appeals to my romantic nature—I cannot help but think of Romeo and Juliet as 'a pair of star-crossed lovers'.

You say 'Forget *Chittacobra*. Remember me.' Yes, yes, I remember every time with you vividly and with joy—but I refuse to forget *Chittacobra*. It does not replace memories of you, but as I said, breathes of you on every page.

Love by email,

K

M@chaurasta.com to K
22 February 2009

Dear K,

Men are so lucky. They have wives to give them children. We poor women have to deliver them ourselves, though I am willing to give men their due in the matter. I don't want you to think that I have anything against my husband. I am grateful for the support he gave me with a bedridden mother and mentally challenged brother.

Talk about troubled waters! Once, twenty-four years ago I remember giving a lecture on the bank of the river Narmada, with the audience sitting on the steps of the ghats and making them quite angry, by criticizing Nehru!

This time I travelled to Panchmarhi along Narmada with three young men and had a whale of a time with them dancing attendance on me.

A Swiss Indologist, who is doing her PhD thesis on *Chittacobra* was here and questioned me so intently and intensely about it that I'm quite sick of it by now. One of the things she asked me was if I had ever regretted writing it, to which I could honestly say, never for a moment. She also asked if the Hindi literary world had ever got around to apologizing for their behaviour to which, unfortunately, I again had to say, no!

Love,

M

K@crossroads.com to M
Mar 7, 2009

Dear M,

Once, long ago, when I was in love with a beautiful girl, I had gone to Panchmarhi by a little train, but unfortunately alone.

The last few days I have not been too well, with a few spells of slight dizziness, and I might eventually have to go in to hospital for a few tests—but not yet. I'll let you know.

Love,

K

M@chaurasta.com to K
8 March 2009

Dearest Kevin,

Never postpone tests. It's not worth it. Feeling dizzy is not good unless with love!

Tell me what does the word 'recantation' bring to mind? I'll tell you later what I need it for, so I don't prejudice you. I need it soon.

Write back.

Maya

`K@crossroads.com` to M
Mar 11, 2009

Maya the magnificent,

Recantation, as I am sure you know, means renouncing, or publicly rejecting, something previously strongly believed. If you are asking about the kind of emotional response the word brings to me, then I think of that dreadful period in Christian history when Catholics and Protestants burned each other at the stake, or the Inquisition tortured people to bring them back to the true faith. Usually, the wretched victims would be offered the possibility even at the last minute, to RECANT— either to save themselves or to be given a quick death. Horrible, but that is the imagery the word conjures up for me—so you see it is a powerful word.

I can't wait to hear why you asked, and how you use it.

I am somewhat better, and hoping to avoid any further problems.

Love,

K

`M@chaurasta.com` to K
11 March 2009

Thanks, Love.

I guess for a non-Christian, the word won't have such a gruesome image! But could not one recant of one's own will? I guess one could, but I don't want to use the word here if it is going to be associated with something that gruesome.

The first part of *Anitya* is called 'The Crossroads' in English. We have yet to name Part 2. In Hindi it's called 'Prati bodh'. The term means rejection of the belief held or path taken earlier, referring to 'Crossroads'.

We thought of 'Insight' or 'Realization', but those are positive terms and the novel ends on a note of unexpressed remorse. So I thought of 'Recantation'. What you said has given me the creeps. I need to rethink! Can you suggest a pithy word to express what I have just explained?

M

K@crossroads.com to M
Mar 11, 2009

M the M—from K the K!

Have been wracking my brains on how to reply to you. I have not come up with much of an answer—but here goes.

First, I may have somewhat overplayed the gruesome bit. I think the real point is that recantation does have something of the sense of renouncing under pressure—Socrates for example.

Recantation is a good strong word, but you must judge whether it fits.

'Transient' is the right word for Anitya in English. Everything passes indeed, except love.

K

M@chaurasta.com to K
12 March 2009

Thanks a ton. You have been a great help .What does the other K stand for?

The theme basically is about disillusionment with oneself, with some degree of guilt involved. Recantation is quite apt, except for its strong religious connotation, because of which my editor seemed to have a slight reservation.

Of course, the perfect title is *Dead End* (particularly in conjunction with Crossroads) but as a title for a novel its offering bait to the critics, sadists as they are and ready to pounce on any pun.

This is fun, almost like talking, the closest I have felt to you for some time.

I might dream of the right word as I sometimes do in the midst of a story.

Bye for now.

Love that may not pass,

M

K@crossroads.com to M
Mar 13, 2009

Krazy! The other K is for Krazy! Yes I agree this is fun. Still no nearer to a helpful idea.

I suppose you may have to leave it to your dreams after all. I will try to join you in them!

Love,

K

M@chaurasta.com to K
14 March 2009

My dream last night said *Counter-Point*. What is your feeling about that?

Maybe I should call it *Anitya the Untranslatable*! A friend of mine used to say, 'while you are searching for the perfect word, the Marwari has made millions.' How true. This is certainly more relaxing and fun than correcting proofs. Can't say if it's more fun than making millions.

So the search goes on.

Love,

M

K@crossroads.com to M
Apr 3, 2009

Here I am, back from bonnie wonderful Scotland in one piece, to the ordinariness of our unfortunate neighbour!

Not much to report. The Scottish Government is asking me to prepare and run an event in the summer on the sovereignty of the people (which Scotland holds as against the English doctrine of the sovereignty of the Crown in Parliament), and I had a number of meetings on that. Also I am involved in a project run by the Herbert Art Gallery and Museum here in Coventry, which aims 'to enhance their collection of art and historical artifacts in the area of conflict, peace and reconciliation.' My task, with others more expert in the art area, is to help them think through just what they are really trying to do and say, before they start seeking or commissioning works.

As always, I look forward to getting your news and doings,

The old Krazy

M@chaurasta.com to K
16 April 2009

Dear K,

Glad you are now an expert on art among other things. But how can you say not much to report, and in the same breath, tell me that the Scottish Government has asked you to prepare and run an event in the summer on the sovereignty of the people. My dear, isn't that an abiding passion of yours! Along with loving me, of course, but I do believe Scotland takes precedence, at least in the arena of action, as it should.

Do keep me posted about the Sovereignty debate.

I am absolutely swamped both on professional and personal fronts. But my heart and mind are always open to news of your other passion, to which mine for writing might bear a pale but intense similarity.

Will write later.

M

K@crossroads.com to M
Apr 20, 2009

Dear M,

Yes, things are happening on the political front and I am trying to be a meaningful part of it. But you are in a different category altogether.

I seem to have a cold I cannot shake off, and a thick head (what's new I hear you say!), and am trying to recover before I go to Iceland in May. Meanwhile keep smiling especially when you think of me—as I do with you.

K

M@chaurasta.com to K
24 April 2009

Dearest,

Ok then, to make you smile with me, I saw a fascinating movie a few days back. It's called *Chaurasta—Crossroads of Love*. It's set in Darjeeling and is in English and Bengali. It starts with an elderly charming man singing Edelweiss in memory of his love, in a voice unbelievably like yours. You can imagine what memories it brought back to me! It was a relaxing, lovely ninety-minute respite.

Write when you can.

Love,

M

K@crossroads.com to M
Apr 24, 2009

Dear Maya,

Sounds fascinating. I must look out for *Chaurasta* if it ever comes this way. I googled but did not get much information. Pity we cannot go to see it together. I love the bit about the charming man singing Edelweiss in memory of his love—but what's new? I know another elderly but very charming man who does the same!

From May 8 to 12 I have to fly to Iceland for some Church events to do with Coventry Cathedral—a long and boring story but I will tell you about it afterwards.

With love,

K

M@chaurasta.com to K
24 April 2009

Dear K,

I couldn't find the film on the web either. But Chaurasta is the main square in Darjeeling and if you just say Chaurasta, the web does yield a few nice photos. The first one is where the movie starts. I guess it's too offbeat to feature on the web.

Have you been to Darjeeling? Somehow, it was jinxed for me. Planned to go many times but could not. Once we had even booked our tickets but something happened to prevent us from going. Now Darjeeling is in turmoil with the Gorkhaland agitation. I met the chief architect of the movement recently and he promised to give me protection should I decide to go there!!

But you are off to Iceland. Darjeeling is tame compared to that. What I can't understand is why you want to avoid hospital tests before going there. To go to Iceland with a cold in the head sounds rather illogical! You should come back with one. So better do the needful.

More later,

M

K@crossroads.com to M
Apr 28, 2009

Dear M,

Yes, I remember Darjeeling clearly and spent a wonderful three months there in 1956, during a gorgeous summer when Kanchenjunga was magnificent. We were at a Bengali Language School learning to make ourselves understood, and reading among other things, the Ramayan in Bengali. The one bad week was in the middle when we had a week's chhuti, and set off in a group on a trek into Sikkim—via Phalut and Sandakphu etc. That week it rained and rained—and the leeches came at us from every corner, almost visibly rejoicing as they sped towards this new and tender blood. Every night in a different dak bungalow, we had to get rid of any that had penetrated our defences —pouring salt on their bloated and satiated bodies!

I remember too the wonderful little train which chugged up from Siliguri to the gloom of Ghoom, before coasting down to Darjeeling. Is it still running? More important, what is happening to Darjeeling? Why would you need a safe conduct to go there? I know little or nothing about Gorkhaland or any trouble? Anyway I hope you get there.

The following year, 1957, we went to Kashmir—Srinagar and Pahalgam I think—also wonderful and also now so sad. But my most intense memories are of course of Delhi and Bombay—and you know why.

As for Iceland etc, my problem is not a cold—that is passing— but occasional slight irregularities of the heart. Not enough to stop me doing anything, but annoying.

How did the elections affect you? They were well reported here, if a little confusingly. What do you think are the prospects now?

With love,

K

M@chaurasta.com to K
6 May 2009

Dearest K,

This should catch you before you leave for Iceland. Take care, keep well. Hope you went to the doctor and are not too bad.

I know you have no interest in that part of my work which has nothing to do with you, but try and read a rather magical story I have sent to Buena Vista, an American website, called 'Seven Little Rooms'.

As for the elections, I am ashamed to admit that I'm a thoroughly rotten citizen. I've not voted since 1993. Now, I just can't seem to get interested in choosing between two equally vile contestants. In fact, since I never informed the authorities about my change of address I'm not on the voter's list for now. Sorry. But of course the Congress is bound to win.

All my love,

Maya (not feeling magnificent at all)

K@crossroads.com to M
May 7, 2009

Dearest,

No. No. It is not true that I am only interested in your work when it involves me. I have also read and appreciated *Country of Goodbyes*—indeed I have it before me right now—though it does say at the bottom 'Kali for Women'—maybe it is not for a mere male like me. In London tomorrow, I have to pick up my copy of *Daffodils on Fire,* which I ordered long ago—it took ages to come. So you see, my love, I am not entirely a self-absorbed philistine!

I leave tomorrow for Iceland, and a few other places, so please don't reply to this until you hear from me again.

You may not feel magnificent—but you are.

Love,

K

K@crossroads.com to M
May 27, 2009

Dearest Maya Maya,

Back from Iceland, but very busy with my book. It was a great experience; a beautiful island, with its strange contrast of glaciers of ice and snow, alongside volcanic springs of boiling water.

While there, I was able to read much of *Daffodils on Fire*. It is wonderful—somehow touched me more than *Kathgulab*, because it breathed you—funny, tragic and full of life. I loved it all, but you cannot blame me if I get a special kind of joy from the parts which bring back vivid memories of a love which was for me, so consuming.

Love,

K

M@chaurasta.com to K
28 May 2009

Dear Love,

It's 10.15 at night. On an impulse I opened the mail and there you were!

Wish I could go somewhere isolated and unfamiliar like Reykjavik. No chance. But one can go anywhere in one's dreams. So, dear love, here's wishing us a shared dream-filled night. I feel you very close to me too at this moment.

Good night.

M

`K@crossroads.com to M`
`Jun 6, 2009`

Dearest,

Nothing much to report—life plods on. Still enjoying *Daffodils*—and through it, you.

Love,

Kevin

`M@chaurasta.com to K`
`6 June 2009`

Dearest,

Nice to open the email for a boring task and find you there! In fact I was thinking of you, not as the boring task, quite separately.

All the best for your book! Hope you hit upon the right publisher soon. It can be such a drag. But aren't you glad at least one phase of the process is over? I tend to celebrate each step. Please let me know the progress of your book and celebrate each step with me.

By the way, they are about to start teaching *Chittacobra* to students learning Hindi in Zurich. Some way to learn Hindi!

Have a nice weekend. Don't plod. Get your hair cut. Sorry if that sounds crazy. You seem to have that effect on me. But I do get my hair trimmed when the 'plodding' gets to me. Sure helps.

Love,

M

K@crossroads.com to M
Jun 6, 2009

Maya Maya,

Thanks for the words of encouragement and strength.

How exciting—*Chittacobra* to be taught in Zurich. Why not persuade them to invite us both for a lecture!

You wanted news from here. So you might have read that the UK is going through a kind of constitutional crisis caused by the ridiculous expenses claimed by many MPs, as revealed by the *Telegraph*.

But closer to my heart and I assume to yours is the news that I might soon depose before the Commission on Scottish Devolution, or the Calman Commission, which was established by the Scottish Parliament in December 2007 and held its first full meeting in April 2008. It has been meeting at roughly monthly intervals. That happened before I finally traced you and wrote to you.

One of its terms of reference was to continue to secure the position of Scotland within the UK. We are debating it again now, though I for one had campaigned for a third alternative to status quo and Independence from the beginning.

I'll send you my wise words after I have said them.

Incidentally, I have been re-reading some of my favourite poems of yours: 'No More', 'A Lament', 'The Night the Cactus Flowered' and your moving story of your own life 'No Amulets Against Lust'. So, you see, you have not been far from my mind and heart.

Love,

K

M@chaurasta.com to K
12 June 2009

My sweet love,

I'll wait with bated breath for your wise words and hope fervently that they influence those you are negotiating with.

I'm in a celebratory mood because I have given the final corrected copy of *Miljul Mann* to the publisher. This letter is a part of that, more so now that I know something momentous is happening in your life. I can sense the anticipation and animation in your emails.

And do you know it is One Whole Year since you re-contacted me. So it's a kind of Anniversary. Happy memories! And a toast to making many more of them!

How's your publisher hunting or sifting going? Tell me all.

With all my love,

M

K@crossroads.com to M
Jun 17, 2009

Dearest Maya,

Amen. Is it really a year since I found you again! I cannot recall the exact day, can you? Maybe we should nominate 1 June, the start of summer, as our official anniversary date!

Congratulations on finishing the new novel. I wish I was there to celebrate with you.

And here is my submission to the Calman Commission. There's hope that negotiation will win the day for us.

The Scottish Constitutional Convention started not with a political goal, but with a fundamental constitutional principle—

the 'Claim of Right for Scotland', which recognized the 'sovereign right of the Scottish people to determine the form of government best suited to their needs'—echoing a constitutional tradition deep in the history of our nation, and implicitly, like the two previous such Claims of 1689 and 1842, denying Westminster's claim to absolute authority. The Convention failed to follow this to its logical conclusion, and inconsistently made constitutional matters a reserved power.

The failure to abide by the principles of the Scottish Claim of Right is the downfall of the Calman Commission. It acknowledged that the Scottish people have the 'sovereign right' to decide the form of government best suited to their needs. That includes independence as well as devolution, so I am disappointed that the Independence option is off your stated agenda. You begin with the premise that Scotland's interests are best served within the union, and that sovereignty lies not with the people, but with Westminster. What good will come out of it when the premise itself is wrong?

Love,

Me

M@chaurasta.com to K
21 June 2009

Dearest,

Your words ring so true and I'm sure, truth shall ultimately prevail. You do believe that, don't you? I do in this case despite my general scepticism.

No I don't remember the exact day, but I do remember it was before 27th of June because that's when my play was first performed and I was deep in its scripting when your mail came out of the blue. Things seem to be coming to a closure in various ways.

The first stage of the Japanese translation of *Kathgulab* is over. It is now with three Jap writers, who are supposed to edit it. They want to call it *Wood Rose* instead of *Kathgulab* as they find that more exotic! Funny! When it was translated in English they found wood rose prosaic!

Now my big news! I have stopped colouring my hair! The new novel shall see a new me! I hope my hair will be a nice salt-and-pepper by the time the book is released. If you like, I'll send you a picture. Hope you succeed in cobbling together a better deal in Scotland than we did with our Independence!

Meanwhile, devolve well, my love and go way beyond it.

M

K@crossroads.com to M
Jun 23, 2009

Dearest M,

First the really big news, alongside which your literary achievements pale into insignificance! You have stopped colouring your hair! Yes, my love, I would love to have a picture.

Good to know that it takes three Japs to deal with the work of one Indian. You have certainly had a busy and fruitful year—it makes me feel very lazy by comparison.

I have decided (unilaterally!) that our anniversary will be June 23—today—because that is Midsummer's Day, and I will always think of *A Midsummer Night's Dream*. OK by you?

With my love,

K

`M@chaurasta.com to K`
`27 June 2009`

Dearest big big news!

I emailed the final draft of the translation of *Anitya*, called 'Anitya Halfway to Nowhere.' to the publisher today! Phew, is it a relief! I celebrated by baking myself a chocolate cake and eating it.

And, of course, the monsoon broke today! Actually there is no 'of course' about it. But somehow it seemed to fit in, as it came late, after awful heat and heartache and with a fair degree of bluster.

How about making 30th June our anniversary? It is a week after the midsummer night, which means the dream was not quite so ephemeral.

In North India, 22nd June is the hottest day of the year and fed up with the heat, all we can think of is the monsoon. Waiting and the final downpour! That's my image of Love!

Maya

`K@crossroads.com to M`
`Jun 30, 2009`

OK my love, 30th it is—so happy anniversary.

I will try to send you a photo—but I am not very good at making this infernal and marvellous machine work for me. Can I post things to you?

I loved you then and I love you now but knew much less of your mind then.

Love,

U No Hoo

M@chaurasta.com to K
5 July 2009

My dearest Love,

Sure you can.

I'm so glad you did not love me for my mind all those years ago. From early childhood, my mind was my refuge from unhappiness, loneliness, pain...whatever! Most people believed that I was perfectly happy living on the level of the intellect and had little passion for anything except reading, and perhaps acting. Good preparation for the future, but still a subterfuge.

So my love, I love you for not discovering the other Maya, whom all others knew. I'm happy with you knowing me, whom only you and I knew. I'm sure the grammar of that sentence is horribly wrong but never mind. You can understand why no one took *Chittacobra* to be a true story!

Off to Simla tomorrow.

With love,

Maya

M@chaurasta.com to K
12 July 2009

Dear K,

Am back from Simla, after a programme at the newly reconstructed Gaiety Theatre.

Where are you? Bit disappointed at not finding a reply on my mail.

`K@crossroads.com to M`
`Jul 16, 2009`

Dear Maya,

I am in sackcloth and ashes! Obviously I did not tell you that I was to be away with the family up north.

I have to confess that my passionate memories of you have little to do with your mind!

But here is my letter to Alex Salmond, First Minister of Scotland to tickle your mind! Remember, you asked for it!

The options for a referendum must not be confined to a choice between Status Quo and Independence. There could be strong support for a third way, which I tentatively call 'secure autonomy'. This gets away from the word 'devolution' which implicitly denies the sovereignty of Scotland's people, but could retain a federal-type presence in a reformed UK. Had the possibility not been vetoed from above, we could have had a vital debate on the wording and implications of such a question. Not only would that have provoked a nation-wide debate, but could have resulted in a well planned consensus. As it is, those who wanted such an option on the ballot, and I suspect they were many, had no choice but to vote for Independence.

Hope you enjoyed Simla—was it a particular play at the reopening? I only once went up to Simla, on a little train—but remember very little about it. Will send a photo and hope it does not put you off too much! What about yours?

K

M@chaurasta.com to K
22 July 2009

Dearest,

I can't help feeling a little anxious. Politics seems to be claiming you again, though negotiating or fighting for Independence is a lot more than politics of the 'UK MPs spending too much' sordid kind.

I loved your letter...I mean to Alex Salmond! What you say about sovereignty resting with the people asserting that rulers, including monarchs, are legitimate primarily due to their consent, you have the support of Gandhi and Tagore. They both rejected the English idea of the Nation because it was an abstraction which, along with sovereignty, lay not in the people, but above them.

I am totally with you, not because I love you, but because I agree with your concept of sovereignty.

But I can feel you drifting away. Now I have to compete not only with your family but also Scotland! Ah, to be in sympathy with one's rival. I can't even complain.

But I'm glad you had a holiday in between. What does up north mean to you? It used to mean Kashmir to us or Scandinavia!

As for Simla there was no play, it was yours truly doing a story-reading at the ugly edifice of Gaiety Theatre. Victorian Gothic architecture if you please. Why it had to be restored at a cost of crores of rupees after being thankfully burnt down just because it happened to be part of our dubious 'heritage', I can't tell you.

The Himachal Culture Ministry had a short story competition. I was one of the three judges. Being newly elected, the govt. decided in its munificence to hold a two-day affair. It was lot of fun, though I hated the vibrations of the theatre. I was told it had a jail for Indian militants in the basement! You can guess my state of mind.

Otherwise, Simla was lovely. We went by taxi (quicker than the little train) from Kalka. It was a welcome break. I spent most of my time, afternoons and evenings drinking! Not much; just enough to put up with Gaiety!

Here are two photos. My hair looks quite black in them but wait another six months!

Love,

M

K@crossroads.com to M
Jul 27, 2009

Dear M,

I am not drifting away from you, love, though yes, I am involved with Scotland's political destiny. Keep busy with it too—am preparing now for the seminar the Scottish Government wants me to chair in November on 'sovereignty'. Glad you sympathize with my other preoccupation but no rival to you, my Maya.

To answer your question... To an establishment Englishman, up north means anything north of Watford gap (a service station on the M1). To a Scot in England, it means north of the border. To a Scot in the central belt of Scotland, it means Inverness or the highlands. Rather illogically in the light of the above, we were away in the Yorkshire Dales—lovely country.

Thanks for the photos. The years have been kind to you—kinder than to me I fear, as you will be able to judge when you get the two I have sent you. I still have the hair, and the eyebrows! But unlike yours, they are white.

Love,

K

M@chaurasta.com to K
3 August 2009

Kevin my love, you sound almost depressed at the idea of time being kind to me. Most people are content to tell me I look even more beautiful now! (ahem)

But seriously, though you didn't say anything to suggest it, I sensed that you were feeling rather low. I hope my picture did not have that effect on you. Is time kinder to me than to you? But of course! I am a woman and have artifice if not art to beat time with. Otherwise time and I have always been at cross purposes.

Anyway, I got your photos. Thanks. Also for the lovely poem at the back and the print of the Cezanne painting. I don't think time has been unkind to you. You look more or less as I described Richard after thirty years in *Chittacobra*, white hair and all. But love, I am glad your eyes are the same as ever and also your mischievous half-smile. I like the more casual of the photographs better.

Mine are definitely at least grey (not my eyebrows though) barring the colour from the bottle, which I've not been using for the last four months. But it needs another six months for it to be properly salt and pepper—or maybe just salt. And of course I always have the option of changing my mind rather than the colour of my hair!

What news about your book? I'll have access to email in Bangalore so if you feel like it, please do write.

Keep well and rest, my love, and may no evil touch you.

Love,

M

K@crossroads.com to M
Aug 3, 2009

Maya,

Wonderful! I had just opened my email when yours popped up! If I sounded a bit depressed it was probably something to do with the fact that the first publisher turned down my masterpiece! Never mind, I have many more to try.

It was certainly nothing to do with your pictures, which are lovely. However, I cannot entirely agree with those who say you are more beautiful than before—but that is probably because my indelible picture of you then is you in my arms, your eyes looking into mine, your face radiating love. Nothing could be more beautiful than that.

Am so glad you were not too much put off by my looks—yes, you did indeed expect Richard to be much like this. Enjoy Bangalore, and have a rest.

I am now starting to write the story of my time at Coventry Cathedral in the '70s—to get this out before November next year, the seventieth anniversary of the destruction of the old Cathedral in 1940.

Love,

K

M@chaurasta.com to K
10 August 2009

Dearest,

I know how it feels to have one's MS returned, but if it's any help—usually other people's experience isn't—it's always the best work which is returned. The mediocre finds immediate acceptance. Hope you'll soon find a publisher.

All the best for all your endeavours; above all, with pushing for sovereignty of the people.

M

K@crossroads.com to M
Aug 20, 2009

Dear Maya,

I have been having dizzy spells, and may have to go in to hospital for tests. I will not be able to use my computer for a while, so please do not send me any mails until I can get back to you.

Love,

Kevin

K@crossroads.com to M
Oct 24, 2009

HAPPY BIRTHDAY

MAYA / MANU

From one whose memories of you are filled with joy at our absorption in each other long ago, pride in your achievements as a writer, and hope that I might have played even a small part in what you have become.

M@chaurasta.com to K
25 October 2009

This is a pleasant surprise and early in the morning! Thank you for remembering and letting me know that Manu is not quite dead.

But much more important, how's your health? I hope the dizzy spells are gone and you don't have to go to the hospital any more. Please take care.

Today was to be an important day. My novel *Miljul Mann*'s book launch was fixed for today, but had to be cancelled because the publisher ended up in the hospital.

Positive: Better him than me! Hence my birthday resolution, to look at the better side even if there isn't any.

Do write to say you are well, at least better.

Maya

M@chaurasta.com to K
21 November 2009

Dear K,

It's been nearly a month since I wrote to you last. Hope you are well. I have been quite worried.

My book launch is at last taking place on 10th December.

M

K@crossroads.com to M
Dec 9, 2009

Dearest M,

I am better. Don't worry. You just give them hell tomorrow! I trust all will go well and you will indeed wow them all.

Sorry I can't be there in the flesh—but you can imagine me in the back row cheering you, and looking a bit smug in the illusion that I might have had a small hand in making you what you are.

Love,

Kevin

`M@chaurasta.com to K`
23 December 2009

Dear Kevin,

Thanks for your wishes for my book launch.

A VERY MERRY CHRISTMAS and HAPPY NEW YEAR to YOU and YOURS.

Anitya Halfway to Nowhere is out.

M

`K@crossroads.com to M`
Dec 23, 2009

Dearest,

A very happy Christmas to you and yours and a good new year in 2010—I am more and more convinced that Copenhagen proves that the present global institutions, political and economic, are simply incapable of tackling the real crisis.

I will get a copy of *Anitya* as soon as I can—and will let you know if I have something to say!!

Love,

Kevin

`M@chaurasta.com to K`
11 February 2010

My dear Kevin,

I am doing a reading from *Anitya Halfway to Nowhere* on Sat 13th in Bangalore. I was hoping you would get to read the book and let me have your reaction some time...whenever... It is in a way my magnum opus! (ahem!) if a lesser mortal like me can lay claim to any such thing...

Hope you are well and in a mood to communicate off and on.

Love,

M

`K@crossroads.com to M`
Feb 12, 2010

Dearest Maya,

Best wishes for the event tomorrow. As usual, I will be quietly sitting in the back row admiring you and listening intently to your voice as you read from your magnum opus—no false modesty please!

I will try to get a copy of *Anitya* from London, and let you have my reactions in due course, though you can hardly expect me to be an unbiased critic!

I have not been too well—getting headaches and slight light-headedness (no comments please) but it has not stopped me from doing things. I have just finished an account of my years at Coventry Cathedral. It runs to 36 pages, but I could bore you with it if you have time. Naturally it leaves out some rather important parts of my life!

Meanwhile, I am sending you the story of the origin of the Cross of Nails which has become the world-wide symbol of Coventry's ministry of peace and reconciliation, as an attachment. I know you'd enjoy reading it.

Love,

Kevin

The Cross of Nails

Four men ensured in 1940 and afterwards that the city of Coventry and its Cathedral would grow into a symbol of peace.

The first, improbably, was called Adolf Hitler. He resolved to make Coventry a symbol of hate and destruction, when he coined and broadcast a new verb, to 'coventrate'(coventrieren in German) and went on to threaten that other British cities would be 'coventrated.' Had he not used these words of hate, the blitz on Coventry would have been listed as one of the comparatively minor episodes of a terrible war. But Hitler unintentionally turned Coventry into an icon. His words had another unintended effect; they fed a desire for revenge which was used to justify terror raids on Germany many times more destructive than the raids on Coventry. It is reported that when the RAF crews who bombed Dresden and Hamburg were asked why, many replied with a single word: 'Coventry'.

The other three men were Jack Forbes, the Rev. A.P. Wales and Richard T. Howard.

Jack Forbes took two charred smoldering beams from the floor of the ruined building, tied them into a cross and placed it on the shattered pile of stones that had been the altar.

Beside it was placed a second Cross that was to become the Cathedral's universal symbol—the Cross of Nails. Rev. A.P Wales took three of the huge ancient medieval nails littering the floor, which had for seven centuries held up the roof. He bound them into a Cross and placed them too on the ruined altar.

Howard's lasting act was to insist that the two words incised on the wall behind the altar in the ruins would be

'Father, Forgive'—not as suggested to him the three words of Jesus from the cross, 'Father Forgive Them.' Forgiveness must not point the finger to others but include the guilt we all share in the sin of the world.

This was the foundation on which the work of rebuilding the Cathedral began from 1970 onwards, with the object of healing the wounds of history. And I am honoured that I played my part in it.

M@chaurasta.com to K
2 February 2010

My dearest K,

I just read in one go your story of the origin of the Cross of Nails! It took my breath away. It was so moving and inspiring. It's strange isn't it, how it always takes a few simple people to undo the harm done by the great or those twisted by power?

I am waiting for the rest of the pages of your account of your days at CC. I am eager to read them, so there is no question of not having time. And yes, I should have asked earlier, but what's happening to the publication of your book? I mean the book on cosmic crisis and creation.

Love,

M

M@chaurasta.com to K
2 March 2010

My dear dear Kevin,

I finally read your memoir of your time in Coventry. You of course write lucidly and from the heart and it really made for easy interesting (digestible!) reading. I am in full sympathy with the idea of the community being bound together and the idea of brotherhood of any kind spearheaded by the church or anyone else.

A very meaningful coincidence happened around the time I read your report/essay. I happened to be in dialogue with an Israeli writer, Judith Rotem, born in Budapest, Hungary. She was taken on the 'Kastner train' to safety as a one-year-old baby, spent several months in Bergen-Belsen, was later in a refugee camp in Switzerland and finally arrived in pre-state Israel at the age of three. Talking to her confirmed my belief that while it's quite impossible for the victim to forget, it is remarkably easy for the perpetrators of injustice/crime/ violence/massacre to do so and cloak their indifference in acts of repentance/reconciliation etc.

When I was in Germany in 1988 and again in 1993, I found the young and middle-aged Germans quite racist and complacent, though we were taken to the concentration camps as a matter of course. But I found it hard to view them as tourist spots. So did my Jewish writer friend from Mexico. Her objection drew the self-righteous indignant response from the Americans, 'Ask the Jews!' When she said she was one, they were speechless.

What hit me was that there was hardly any evidence of repentance or desire for a change of attitude.

I had gone immediately after the fall of the Berlin Wall in 1993 and was forever warned by people in West Berlin not to go to East Berlin as they were all thieves! (naturally being poorer!) I spent a lot of time in East Berlin, as most of the museums and opera houses were there. I found the people much more warm-hearted, with a far greater sense of humour than the West Berliners. Perhaps because they were as poor as I was, or almost!

I can't help but wonder why the British don't talk or write about the atrocities they committed in India (the Andaman prisons etc) which happened at the same time as Hitler, with equal repentance?

But that is cerebral quibbling. Personally I want to wish you success from my heart in your endeavour to continue to unite and reconcile Europe, and also improve and unite the local community in equality and amity, the way you did in the seventies.

I am truly impressed by the way Coventry Cathedral was resurrected and by your and its endeavours for Peace. Equally impressed by the heart-felt lucid writing about it by you, dear heart.

I am sorry for being a skeptic about true repentance and healing the wounds of history, but History and Copenhagen are on my side.

With love and memories, which you may now want to invoke and now not.

On a lighter plane, the way you want to run our relationship reminds me irreverently of a ration shop! What we in India euphemistically call a Fair Price Shop, where nothing is fair. Everything in limited quantities and fixed quota, if and when available. Sorry, but the image was just too strong and funny to keep to myself.

Love again,

Maya

Better send this before I delete it as I have a few other messages to reply to.

K@crossroads.com to M
Mar 3, 2010

Dear Maya,

Your comments on my memoir of the time in Coventry do raise some questions for me. When it comes to India, I confess to being ambivalent. I loved India—partly at least because I found and loved you. I do recognize the atrocities that shame us as a nation, and how easy it is to forget, but I am not ready to compare that in any way with the 'greatest criminal conspiracy in history', that of the Nazi regime.

I recognize that Britain did not come to India for altruistic reasons or for anything but selfish motives, and that there is much for which to be ashamed. But I do believe that British rule did bring much that was good in its time. And that it remains amazing, as one historian put it 'that so few ruled so many for so long with such little use of force.'

I would love to be there to see your reactions to that.

Anyway, don't be too hard on me! And maybe share some of the memories.

With love,

Kevin

M@chaurasta.com to K
3 March 2010

Dearest Kevin,

My only objection, and my Jewish friend's too, to being taken to the concentration camps was their expectation that we would be totally blown away by their repentance and ready to believe in their benevolence now. I have no belief in historians and their platitudes—particularly not in those of the Raj in India.

As everyone knows, history is written by the victors from different individual viewpoints, and its only after one has read a whole lot of partial lies that one can know a partial truth. Literature helps, as it is written by ordinary people, or the losers if you like!

When and if you read *Anitya*, you'll find that one of the most evolved and sensitive characters in it is British, one Marshall. Actually I had met someone like him as a child (lest you think he is modelled on you!) But frankly, loving you must have had something to do with my choosing to write about him with so much feeling. It was written in 1980 a year after *Chittacobra* so you were very much in my mind.

As for your quote, tell me, just how much force can one use against a people who refuse to resist with any force, thanks to Gandhi? However, whenever there was the slightest show of force by Indians, the retaliation was cruel and extreme, whether in 1857 or 1931 or 1942.

I never for a moment intended to put it on par with Hitler's planned genocide. But a bigger evil does not mean a lesser one can be forgotten or believed to be partially beneficial.

I was not being hard on you. I am happy for all of you in Europe for having moved on. I was just sharing my experiences and thoughts, naturally so very different from yours.

To hell with it all! Just forget it, love. Please let's not make the political quite that personal! Anyway as you are in no way responsible for what happened as far as Britain and India are concerned, I don't see why you need to defend the British rule.

With lots of love (is that permitted in the ration shop today?)

Maya

K@crossroads.com to M
Mar 10, 2010

Dear Maya, always Maya.

Thanks for your thoughts, which are always stimulating and challenging. I would love to discuss them with you, but have a problem.

For the last few days I have been having increased spells of light-headedness with heart irregularity, which means I may have to go into a hospital. I am becoming more aware of my own mortality. So, very reluctantly I need to ask you to stop our contact, until I know more. I am sorry, but I fear my family knowing, as they would have access to my computer.

Reply to this, if only to tell me I am stupid and selfish. But after that, let it be for a while; a fast rather than a ration!

With love,

K or R

M@chaurasta.com to K
11 March 2010

My dear sweet love,

God bless you. Why should I call you stupid or selfish? You are only preparing for the inevitable eventuality, which though seemingly opposed to Life is very much a part of Life. A great Urdu poet once said: why would I mind dying if it was only once? Also, the day of death is pre-ordained so why lose sleep over it? That's the sense of the couplets; I am not going to impose the originals upon you.

But I'll continue to pray that you come out victorious in your battle with mortality and are on your feet for some more years to come.

Don't worry about your family having access to your mail. All you have to do is to delete me from the inbox, sent mail and contacts.

I was going to write to you that it was stupid to argue about history when we were about to become history ourselves, when your mail came. Sorry to sound flippant but irony is the best weapon against pain. Bless you again.

Love,

Maya, all Maya

M@chaurasta.com to K
14 June 2014

Dearest K,

I know I am not supposed to write to you. God, that sounds awful as if I am under some kind of sentence or penance. Better say we are not supposed to correspond via email. But I could not help following avidly the upcoming Referendum for an Independent Scottish Parliament on the web. During the process I often felt impelled to write to you, but desisted.

Today is one of those days. I want to applaud you for what you have written. It is so much after my heart.

What infernal and breath-taking cheek. Cameron tells us Scotland would have to join a queue to get into the EU which he seems so keen on getting out of. It is of course nonsense to believe the EU would keep Scotland out after the democratic vote of a prosperous stable nation, which already has so many ties with Europe. Even if it were true—which it is not—we would be on the way in—and pass him on his way out! What we must not do, is to allow him to drag us out of Europe against our will. Could there be a better example of why independence is vital if we are to make our own relationships, and decide ourselves where and when sovereignty should be shared in a spirit of true interdependence. I repeat: What infernal cheek.

Carry on love, in the same vein. And don't worry. You're safe. I am not going to press 'send' to this mail. It shall remain in my drafts and who knows...maybe...one day...you'll see it.

M@chaurasta.com to K
16 June 2014

Dear K,

Here I am, again moved by your soul-stirring speech!

Dear citizens of Scotland, We stand at a crossroads of history and the way we choose will shape the lives of all of us for generations to come. Whichever road we take, we can be proud of the way the whole nation has been set alight. People who in the past saw no point in voting have become deeply and intelligently involved in the debate. Scotland as a nation has awakened—and I do not think we will go back to sleep. Why is this? A taxi driver in Edinburgh gave me the answer: 'We are alive. For the first time, people really believe it is they who decide.'

Whatever we decide, we must forge a new unity in our beloved Scotland and not lose the unbelievable energy and commitment that has been built up these last months. I have no right to tell you what to do in the vote on Independence of Scotland, but maybe from my own experience, I might be able to clarify what this is all about and help those who are still confused by the conflicting messages we receive every day. I am not a politician. I am not a member of any party. I am a Patriot but not a Nationalist.

Just my sentiments! For long I have said that I am a Patriot but not a Nationalist, and annoyed hordes of people. But in your case it takes on a more vital meaning. You have given up a politician's slogan-mongering for the real thing. More power to you!

But the eternal cynic that I am, I have to say one thing. I do hope the other Scots feel as passionately about Independence as you do. There is always a great danger that a majority of people would start calculating the benefits or otherwise of Independence and staying within the fold under someone's protection. We in India went with primal passion. Gandhi said, 'Go and leave us to our devices.' If we have to suffer so be it, we would still be free!

Hope the Scots opt for Independence and not well-being.

Again, this mail shall remain in my drafts till I decide to send it. I can't promise any particular date for doing or not doing it but I realize you are totally absorbed in the Referendum so I'll not intrude...till...whenever.

M@chaurasta.com to K
18 September 2014

Oh my dear love. I am so sorry for the No to the Referendum!

I can't abide by the 'ration' any more. I have to send you this mail to tell you again, though you know it well, that I not only love you but your aspirations.

Someday...sooner than later...I do firmly believe that you will have your Independence just as we had ours. That 55 percent of Scots will not calculate the benefits of Independence but risk it at whatever price!

Till then...Remember I love you and believe in you.

I am enclosing the earlier two mails I had in my drafts since June 2014. Why? I do not know—unless it's to bolster my belief and yours in my love, and in your own belief.

With Love Forever,

Maya

K@crossroads .com to M
Oct 12, 2014

Dear M,

You have been on my conscience for days, and I was well aware I missed answering your warm mail for almost a month.

Lynda died suddenly and totally unexpectedly three weeks ago, and the girls and I have been dealing not just with grief, but with all the things that had to be done. I simply have not got to my computer

That part of my life is sadly over—but we are not.

Love,

K

M@chaurasta.com to K
12 October 2014

Oh my God, I'm so very sorry.

I can understand and empathize.

My love and condolences.

M

`K@crossroads.com to M`
Nov 2, 2014

Thank you. I'm getting back to work slowly. There is so much happening. I'll contact you soon.

K

`K@crossroads.com to M`
May 9, 2015

Dearest Maya,

Here are my thoughts on the just concluded elections in the UK. I'm sure you'll share both my joy and my misgivings.

The UK has just gone through an election which may well shake our nations to the core. We have a clear division between England, where the Conservatives under Cameron soundly defeated Labour, and Scotland, where the Scottish National Party (SNP) almost miraculously won 56 of the 59 seats. The last three were one each for Conservative, Labour and Liberal, leading one paper to joke that each party had fewer MPs than the two pandas in Scotland!

More important, there is a profound political and ideological gulf. Many are suggesting that this situation, along with the growing phenomenon of English nationalism, could lead to the break-up of the UK. I believe that it can be avoided if there is a radical reform of the archaic UK electoral and political system. It is time to move to a Federal system.

I'll be busy in the next few weeks working on this solution, with trust in your love and support.

Keep well my love. I'll be back soon.

Kevin

M@chaurasta.com to K
7 July 2015

Dearest Kevin,

You must be busy with work, particularly the political ramifications of the election results. And hopefully a new Referendum for an Independent Scottish Parliament. But I thought I'll give you this news. I have redone the MS of *The Last Email* and sent it to the publisher! I have made a whole lot of additions, but once you start writing. it takes on a life of its own. So...

I was rather ill, so my son insisted I come to Bangalore to be cared for. During my fortnight here, I thought I might as well finish the book, having worked obsessively on it earlier.

Love,

Maya

M@chaurasta.com to K
16 July 2015

Dearest Love,

It is early morning. And it's pouring; raining heaven hard!

I woke up suddenly thinking of you and realized there was something I needed to do.

So here it is. I'm sending you the complete manuscript of *The Last Email*.

Since I have added a lot about Scotland, please read it and see if there is any bit you want to be changed, deleted etc.

Don't take too long love, if possible, to say OK.

This MS has been prepared through three major illnesses. Strange! Guess the intensity came from them. But now I need to rest a while.

Stranger yet, I love you still with almost the same passion, tempered of course by what my meagre body can sustain.

Hoping you are well, despite all the terror strikes not only in Dhaka and Kashmir but Europe as well.

With all my love and a belief in yours,

M

K@crossroads.com to M
Jul 20, 2015

Dear M,

I do hope you are feeling perfectly alright now. I'll try not to take too long, but bear with me.

K

K@crossroads.com to M
Aug 8, 2015

Dear M,

I look forward more and more to the new book, which has the potential to cause quite a stir—especially if others have been asking the same question as your PhD on *Chittacobra* student.

I am sorry for being so long in replying, but I have been suffering from a very unpleasant bout of atrial fibrillation. Maybe you are still affecting my heart!

I must be honest—after Lynda's death I still cannot change my recognition that she was the love of my life and of course the mother of my three lovely daughters. This in no way diminishes what I feel for you, but as you know it has always been in the background of our relationship, and accounts for at least some of my crazy behaviour to you over the years.

Maybe *The Last Email* will show that sense of ambivalence.

With my love,

K

M@chaurasta.com to K
14 August 2015

Dear K,

I'm glad Lynda was the love of your life and you had a long and fruitful life with her. Few people are so lucky. I'm truly sorry for your loss and understand how you must miss her.

But I must say that our on-and-off interlude had nothing to do with Lynda or Naveen, my husband, who I can't say was the love of my life.

The loves of my life are my sons—but that's a very private domain.

Our relationship, by whatever name you call it, was without reference to anyone but us.

So...you don't have to justify, apologize or explain. Your ambivalence is already well recorded.

But strangely I have been feeling since Lynda's death that our tenuous relationship would soon end too. However ironical, it seems fated, and in a weird way, befitting, so much so that I almost feel no regret. I do feel that the time has come for us to stop living a memory.

M

K@crossroads.com to M
Aug 24, 2015

My dear dear Maya,

What can I say...but this...

Three Wise Women

Would have asked directions

Arrived on time

Helped deliver the baby

Brought practical gifts

Cleaned the stable

Made a casserole

And there would be

Peace on earth.

In other words

They would not have dithered!

Forever,

K